For Tracey.
Hope you enjoy
this book.
Best wishes!
Thomas McKinley
6.7.24

TALES OF MYKONOS

ANCIENT MYTHS RETOLD
ON A MODERN GREEK ISLAND

THOMAS MCKNIGHT

Published in the United States and the United Kingdom by Polia Press, Litchfield, CT

ISBN 978-1-63683-065-0 (pbk.)
ISBN 978-1-63683-490-0 (hardcover)
ISBN 978-1-63683-947-9 (ebk.)

Printed in the United States of America

POLIA · PRESS

ACKNOWLEDGMENTS

Besides my wife Renate who provides the music to my life and makes all things possible. I want to thank Patrick Cline, a consummate editor and David Carroll who, for an author too old for the internet; typed and retyped the results of all this editing.

DEDICATION

Within eyesight of the birthplace of Apollo and Artemis I met my own fated muse and constant companion at breakfast on a sunny July morning. Her name Renate means rebirth and this book is dedicated to her.

TABLE OF CONTENTS

Preface ix

1. The Centaur 1
2. Daphnis 14
3. The Last Priest of Isis 26
4. The Beautiful Boy 42
5. Last of the Ghisi 52
6. Return of Apollo 70
7. Andromeda 87
8. Circe 98
9. Nymphs of Mykonos 106
10. Return of Odysseus 116
11. The Black Caique 123
12. Judgment of Paris 138
13. A Kouros 147
14. Blind Love 160

PREFACE

"I have just come across the most astounding discovery!"
"And what could that be?" asked Angelos, my oldest friend on the Greek island of Mykonos as we sat at the Kastro Bar.

"You know there are a thousand theories about the location of Atlantis or even whether it actually existed. Now someone called Christos Djonis has overlaid Plato's precise description on a real map and presto – he has found it in plain sight. When Plato said it existed the sea level was 400 feet lower. Take away that much water and the Cyclades form one big island. Mykonos and the others are just the mountain tops of Atlantis. Santorini or Thera a few miles offshore fits Plato's description of its capital with its concentric protected harbor. When the volcano that is Thera blew up the Minoan civilization about 1200 BC that was just the latest of many other disasters going back millennia to the earlier time Plato writes about.

"Is that the siren song that makes people like you return again and again? You all had previous lives on Atlantis?" Angelos said and laughed.

"It could be, but in this lifetime Mykonos represented my youth when there was magic in the air. Everything was in the future, still possible."

"I was born here and it was magic for me, too," Angelos said and took a sip of his ouzo. "But it isn't the same place anymore and we aren't young either."

When I first arrived in the seventies of the last century it was an island for romantics who did not feel altogether comfortable in the modern world, where one could step back and enjoy the primal pleasures of sun and sea and dancing under the stars at night. Today it has joined the world with a modern airport offering direct flights from everywhere, highways, a cruise boat marina, and five star hotels but then there were still corners where one could calmly ruminate over the passage of time.

One was the Kastro Bar – so called because its location in the oldest part of the port used to be a Venetian castle. Next door is the Paraportiani, a conglomeration of chapels whitewashed so often they appear to be melted on the edges like ice cream, extolled in books as the epitome of Cycladic island architecture. At sundown the Kastro was filled with haunting music that evokes the brief flare of summer and fleshly beauty, the arrival of night; Satie's Gymnopedie, Maria Callas arias from Bellini, the Four Last Songs of Richard Strauss. Patrons stared out to sea like people in a Hopper painting, conversing quietly so as not to spoil the overall mood of sweet melancholy.

When Angelos and I stayed late and drank too many mojitos we watched the moon rising over the port's signature windmills, in one of which he lived. Before tourism hit the island, his family was considered unfortunate in their inherited acres – not in the fertile inland countryside but on rocky cliffs facing the Aegean accessible only by donkeys. Those precipices now form the foundations of sprawling villas with infinity pools. This enabled him to retire early, and since his ambitions were modest, had no children and a wife who'd died young, he was left with an inordinate amount of time to socialize, read and sleep during the day, and observe the scene in bars and tavernas after night falls.

We met each other chasing women on Elia Beach when no one wore clothes. "Angelos Angelopoulos," he said offering his hand to me as we sprawled on mats ogling a trio of beauties who had spread a large beach blanket between the water and us. Although we didn't find romance that day (the girls turned out to be lesbians) Angelos and I became fast friends. It helped that we were not competitive – he studied architecture although he never practiced and I was on my way to becoming an artist. More importantly our preferences in women ran in opposite directions. He was partial to zaftig figures, a taste I tease him must have been inherited from Turkish harems, while I was usually smitten by lithe young creatures who didn't need bras.

Often over the years he became a perfect foil as we gossip and reminisce about the past, real or imaginary. Sometimes the stories we spin begin to resonate and rhyme with tales of the ancient gods, especially when they involve artists and their muses and take place on this island haunted by antiquity, where centaurs still roam and Andromeda still lives.

THE CENTAUR

Just after sunset Angelos and I found ourselves at Apostoli's, one of the string of tavernas that surround the main plaza of Ano Mera, the one village in the interior of the island of Mykonos. As twilight descended, swallows swooped low hunting insects and children played noisily at soccer and hide-and-go-seek.

Built around the island's largest monastery housing no more than several monks these days and near a convent with one nun left, Ano Mera has never been a tourist draw like the port. It comes alive on one weekend in mid-August for the Panagyra, a festival honoring Mary *Stella Maris* which some scholars say replaced a celebration in classical times that honored all the gods. Then its tavernas are lit, the bazouki plays and there is dancing in the streets.

We were partaking of *mezes* – the plates of cheese, olives and small tomatoes that traditionally accompany the ouzos we had ordered – when our attention was drawn to an elegant older gentleman who negotiating his entrance with a cane, sat down at a table next to ours. All three of us nodded hello and the man ordered an ouzo too, in English with a French accent.

"Have you been to Mykonos before?" Angelos asked raising his glass as if to toast the stranger.

"Yes, I spent one summer here more years ago than I care to remember."

"Did you enjoy it then?" I asked.

"Yes and no," the old man said. "Of course I was young and had no trouble with my knees or anything else," he continued with a smile as he brandished his cane. "But I almost died here."

"Whatever happened?" Angelos asked.

"If I recount it, you will find it hard to believe. It happened in the ruins of the castle," he said pointing to a hill behind us that loomed over the village.

"Please tell," Angelos said, impatience in his voice.

The old man put up his palm. "We have time, especially when one is as old as I am. Much time."

Back then as you may remember, Mykonos was undiscovered by the wide world except by café society stopping for the day on yachts. Have you ever seen that famous photo of Cole Porter with a wry smile as he mounts a donkey to ride up to the windmills? Visitors then like me were mostly French. One had established an art school, which attracted rich Greeks with nothing else to do. Nobody became famous. I was an art student myself at that time, and managed to live poorly but well enough with the help of a small inheritance. Unlike my father who had been consumed by the arts of war (he was a colonel under de Gaulle) I decided to devote myself to the finer arts.

After my first desolate winter in Paris as a student sketching plaster copies of classical statues, or naked models with unclassical udders, spring arrived as splendidly as it does in the Ile-de-France, accompanied by a fever to discover what lay beyond the horizon.

One leaf-dappled morning as I strolled along the Seine as it flows by the *Quartier Latin*, my eyes were attracted to a watercolor flapping from the booth of one of the many booksellers displaying their wares. It was simple, almost like an architect's drawing, more white than blue and depicted a church I later learned was called the Paraportiani in Mykonos.

"Monsieur Tourté is very well-known in Greece. He makes postcards of his views of the Cycladic islands. This is an original *aquarelle* by him," said the *bouquinist*.

I happily paid him the few francs he demanded, and in June inspired by my purchase I found myself standing in the same place Tourté had painted my picture. I found Chora, the port of Mykonos, was a symphony of cube-like houses laid out higgledy-piggledy along twisted lanes to slow the north winds blowing in from the indigo-colored Aegean.

The town was made for artists – a full palette of whites with enlivening touches of bouganvillea purple, oleander pink, and deep pine green. A few Venetian red domes of churches punctuated the labyrinth. The dry rocky island was sprinkled with white farmhouses over a landscape colored the ochre of a lion's pelt.

As you may remember in those days its poor inhabitants rented out spare rooms for a pittance to tourists like me, and caiques left the harbor every morning to take us to the beaches, especially those that allowed nude bathing. After a day of nakedness in the sun, wearing no more than a sarong for lunch at a seaside taverna and after a siesta back in town, we foreigners congregated at bars and restaurants in the cool of the evening when the wind died down. Later we danced the night away at discos — first the Nine Muses, and after midnight at Remezzo.

It was a life so pleasant and easy that many would-be artists and writers simply got stuck in its rhythm like a stylus endlessly repeating the same notes on a phonograph and never engaging in their arts. I was more determined. Every morning I wandered with my sketchbook. While late-sleeping tourists were not yet awake, the town bustled with donkeys saddled with panniers of vegetables, and locals stocking up shops and tavernas. Two competing bakeries pumped wonderful aromas into the street where I stopped daily for a croissant to munch with a sludgy Greek coffee I'd buy at a café on the port. My morning entertainment was watching the ferry from Athens arrive with hoarse bleats, or observing Petros the Pelican, scavenge at the fish market on the waterfront.

Soon my sketchbooks were filled with enough details to inspire me through the next winter's painting in Paris. Enough of decrepit nudes and casts of Greek statues. I would make famous (and make myself famous) off the sun-warmed walls of the Aegean.

By this time I had made some friends. One of them, Sebastian de la Salle, an elegant denizen of the seventeenth *arrondissement* in Paris came from a family that prospered during the war selling electrical generators to all sides. His father had connections to the Vichy government, and his uncle in exile in London was married to a relative of de Gaulle. Considering my father's connection to "Le Grand Charles" that was our initial bond. Sebastian was probably what I would have turned out to be had I his generous allowance. He used his art — which wasn't very good — as an excuse to hang out with habitués of the art academy. His true metier was gossip, along with a knack for telling convoluted and embellished stories. His trademark was a volume of Proust that he carried but seldom read in his beach bag.

4

"Have you heard about the centaur that lives in Ano Mera?" he asked me one day as we lay on our straw mats on Elia Beach. I laughed. "Probably a deformed donkey, but you never know," he said with a suave grin. "Some say 'centaur' is a local figure of speech for 'lunatic.'" I'd never been to Ano Mera but I was always up for adventure and his comment intrigued me.

Instead of the usual caique, Sebastian preferred to be driven to the beach in one of the island's fourteen taxis that bumped along the few roughly paved roads on the island. To ensure the taxi would return you to town, you did not pay until the round trip was completed.

A few of us defrayed the cost by car pooling and the next morning I had the taxi driver drop me off in Ano Mera on the way to the beach. Although there were already several simple tavernas around its main square then alongside the monastery with its pretty Venetian-style belfry, it was still a farming village where one could hear cocks crowing and pigs grunting no matter where you were.

After a brief reconnaissance, I walked up the hill crowned by the ruins of the Venetian castle. On the way, next to the convent inhabited then by two nuns, I rested under a spreading eucalyptus tree, unpacked a cheese pie and opened my thermos filled with Fix beer.

As wasps buzzed around my leftovers, I crumbled a leaf from the tree above to release its invigorating aroma, and stumbled the rest of the way to the summit where I fell asleep on a stone bench in the shade of a small padlocked chapel.

I awoke to a face staring down at me.

"You cannot stay," she said in sing-song. "You must go."

She was beautiful in an equine way—a prominent straight nose, and the glossy black hair of a horse's mane. I smiled as she skittered away and didn't believe a word of what she said.

The view from on top encompassed the island in all four

directions. Its sere rounded hills appeared like random cogs between which lay the dark blue sea. Gray smears on the horizon—Naxos, Paros, Delos, Tinos, were islands of legend. Theseus of the dark sails, birthplace of Apollo and Artemis, the wonder-working icon of the Virgin on Tinos.

I sketched for an hour or two in silence, broken only by tinkling goat bells and breezy zephyrs eddying in from the north. I could see the entire village just below me. Not a soul was visible – it was the afternoon siesta. I wondered, what happened to the girl? How old was she? What kind of life was it to live here?

Later that afternoon Sebastian's taxi picked me up at the roadside on its way back to town. Sebastian sat in the backseat, bookended by two stylish French girls he'd met on the beach. Both wore batik sarongs that elaborately wrapped their brown bodies—ready for adventure, which we had that evening.

The next morning all four of us taxied to Elia Beach where we spread our towels under a straw umbrella next to Yanni's Taverna. He had a French wife who made a perfect *tarte tatin* daily along with the usual moussakas and souvlakis. The girls felt like ouzo so we drank ourselves silly before a post-prandial nap on the beach.

We were awakened by the cry of *"Karpouzi, Karpouzi."*

A donkey had arrived laden with watermelons and surrounded by three black-clad peasant women and a grizzled man wearing the ubiquitous Greek captain's hat. What made it a tableau from a classical painting by an artist like Poussin was the contrast with their bronzed customers. A beautiful boy just beyond teenage wore nothing but a wide brimmed straw hat – add feathered wings to it, and he could have been Hermes. One of the women might have been my equine friend - I wasn't sure because a black kerchief obscured most of her face but her staring eyes looked familiar. When I arose and approached to buy a wedge of the succulent fruit, I forgot that I lacked clothes and she turned away.

We ditched the French girls by evening. Sebastian felt they

were freeloaders and that night we followed the usual tourist circuit from bar to bar, a bite to eat, then disco to disco.

In those days there was a bazouki place a bit outside of town, accessible only by taxi. Unlike the discos, it catered mainly to Greeks who worked up to a frenzy dancing over broken plates and even glasses that accompanied whining, wailing music as the night slid downhill to dawn. Sebastian decided it would be fun to go there, and so after midnight we shared a taxi with a Greek couple. When we arrived, plates were already flying. A group of men holding each other's shoulders leaped and curtsied in a wavering line – a descendant of the crane dance first performed at classical festivities on Delos I'd been told. Later, a waiter balanced a table in his teeth, atop of which was a goblet of precariously shaking water. All the entertainers were male until a dark complected girl appeared. Heavily made up with hennaed eyes, she wore a head scarf that sparkled with fake gold coins and flowing dark veils. She danced like a dervish – her ankle bracelet glittered and her movements increased in velocity as drachma notes rained down. Her penultimate dark veil was whipped off and she was left wearing just a virginal white one that I imagined I could see through. When she finished to a final cloudburst of cash and plates, she donned one of the discarded black veils and picked up the others along with her loot.

Sebastian beckoned to her holding up a sheaf of banknotes. She tiptoed over through the shards of glass and pottery and stared at me. I realized that beneath the war paint she was the equine girl I had already met.

"Would you like a drink?" I asked.

She wagged her finger "no," but came and sat next to me anyway. She finally accepted a glass of soda. She was panting, and the perfume of her body mingled with sweat was overwhelming. I tried to make conversation, but didn't get beyond, "You're very good" before she put her finger on my lips and leaned into my ear.

"*Avraio*, meet me twelfth hour at place where I see you." For the first time she smiled. "I like to show you."

"Night or day?" I asked.

"Night, night," she replied, stood up and disappeared behind the bar.

"What was that all about?" Sebastian asked me.

When I told him, he suggested it might not be personal. "Maybe she has a brother or father who plans to rob you. It might be more of an adventure than you bargained for." I barely listened. *You're just jealous* I thought.

Avraio, the next day, I prevailed upon a taxi driver to drop me at midnight next to the convent in Ano Mera. He made a joke about services with the ancient nuns.

On the advice of Sebastian, I left my valuables and most of my money at home. What I had was rolled into a small leather pouch (stylish then) that hung around my neck. This was before electricity had reached most of the island outside of the port, and after the taxi drove away I was surrounded by darkness lightened only by a full moon, which dappled the ground through the leaves of the giant eucalyptus tree.

"You came. Good," she said, her hand grasping my wrist and without preamble, nuzzled up to me. She motioned for me to sit on a stone bench outside the chapel.

"I dance, just for you," she said as she arose and whirled around pantomiming the dance of the seven veils I'd seen before. I was transfixed like watching a cobra as her lithe body swayed in the moonlight. When I saw that it culminated this time with all the veils removed, my fascination became physical. Even in the dark I could make out her eyes staring at me. I wondered what would happen next. She was an island girl acting out of character. She sat down again and took my hand.

"I see you. I like you," she said.

I wrapped my arms around her damp body.

"Not now," she said and wriggled away. "You also. We run to beach. My sport."

It took a while for this to sink in.

"Quick. People sleep," she added, as she dressed in the dark.

Soon I was following her barefoot figure silhouetted by the moon, now a pale orange disc descending towards Athens and the west. Pumping muscle. A light breeze tickling and cooling my body.

It was a mile or so to the shore where she quickly shed her garments, except for a curious belt that holstered a Pan's pipe, and splashed directly into the dark sea. Molten silver waves, phosphorescent shadows. All the clichés of romantic movies. The lights of an inter-island ferry rode the horizon like a caterpillar far out to sea. The girl whose name I still did not know pointed at it. "It goes to Rhodos."

Afterwards we lay on the tiny pebbles that stood in for sand. She threw her cold body, naked except for her belt, on top of me.

"Warm" she said and we made love.

We ran and walked back but not nearly as fast. Twice we hid behind a wall, once in the shadow of a tree as we sensed something moving. A cock crowed out-of-sync with the dawn. When we arrived at the eucalyptus tree, I asked for her name. She put a finger to her lips.

"I at least need to know your name."

Without answering she strolled into the night. There was no question of available transportation at that hour but halfway into the five mile hike to the port, I managed to hitchhike a ride on one of the noisy three-wheel motorized carts farmers used to deliver produce and fell asleep in my room—spent, as they say in old novels.

The next morning Sebastian barely believed me.

"It is so out-of-character for an island girl to act that way, perhaps she is a *putain* from Athens."

9

"She didn't ask me for drachmas," I replied.

"Maybe you'll pay some other way."

I looked for her at the bazouki club that night but she was not there. When I asked the bartender when she would appear, he acted as if he'd never heard of her.

The day after that I visited the eucalyptus tree and, in fractured Greek, asked a passing farmer on a donkey if a girl lived nearby. He looked at me blankly, then smiled revealing old gold teeth and said "*Yasoo*," the greeting hereabouts, and rode on. I was obsessed. Had it really happened? I thought I heard a bellow from a nearby shed, but was that a dream too?

Later I scanned the crowd of locals performing the evening *passagiatta* in front of the cafes lining the town's waterfront. Many of the girls looked somewhat like her – the gene pool of the natives on a small island is limited in scope – but no one had her intense eyes. I asked again at the club. The bartender replied "M'sieu, m'sieu," and offered me an ouzo.

At midnight I found my taxi man again and we sputtered out into the dark countryside. I sat for awhile under the eucalyptus tree hoping she would miraculously appear. Again I heard a bellow – like a bull – but this time far away in the direction of the Venetian citadel. The moon, still full, was bright enough to guide my path up the side of the hill. Pebbles and potshards clattered down as I climbed. When I reached the summit I scanned the more-or-less level plateau pockmarked with low thistled bushes. A small white-washed chapel in the middle hid something happening on the other side. A light breeze brought the sound of piping, a simple melody in an ancient key. I thought of the girl's Pan's pipe.

I crept closer and edged my head around the chapel's wall.

What I saw was like encountering a live dinosaur or a knight in full armor. Bareback atop a beast with a man's torso and bearded head was the object of my search, wearing what appeared to be the fleecy hide of a sheep cinched by that belt she had never removed

10

even when we made love. As she piped, the centaur performed a kind of dressage with its hoofs, pawing the ground and side stepping like a trained Lippizaner.

The centaur saw me first, turned its head and bellowed. The girl alarmed, stared in my direction. She dismounted and the centaur pawed the ground behind her.

"Go away. Never tell or you will die." She gripped both of my arms – her eyes flashing. "Go now. Quickly."

The centaur seemed to be ready to explode.

"Go, go," she said and pushed me from the back. I stumbled back down the hill – fear overtaking fascination at the bizarre sight or my feeling for the girl. I walked back into a town that still lay abed, perhaps dreaming of the very things I'd seen in real life.

After a long sleep myself, Sebastian knocked on my door to tell me he was heading for the beach. "You won't believe this," I began and told him what had happened forgetting to mention the girl's proscription not to do just that. A sophisticated smirk on his face made his doubts clear even as I spoke.

When he left I drew from memory, in as much elaborate detail as I could remember the centaur with its fleece-clad rider. I must say it turned out to be one of my better efforts and I proudly showed it to Sebastian late that afternoon at a waterfront café where he was ensconced with new friends from the beach. He held it up to show his entourage.

"Look, my artist friend has captured in his drawing big game, a real live centaur," he said. "And a girl too."

I tried to retrieve the drawing from Sebastian but I was too slow as he moved close to a nearby table populated by grizzled farmers in from the countryside for a chat, an ouzo, and to ogle lightly-clad tourists.

"Excuse me gentlemen, have you seen this centaur in Ano Mera?" Sebastian joked. One put a hand over his eyes. The others stared. "I guess they are the wrong people to ask for artistic opinions," Sebastian said as he gave the drawing back. "I'll buy it when you decide to sell."

That evening when I returned to my room a note appeared on the bed. Written on a grimy torn-off piece of the rag paper I use for watercolors was a short note in a hand not used to the western alphabet.

"I want see you. Come tonight." That was all, but I knew exactly what it meant.

With a mix of fascination, fear and trepidation not finding her under the tree I again mounted the hill, again heard the pipes and a bellow. When I peered around the wall, the girl saw me immediately.

"Come" she beckoned from astride the centaur. "He is my father. I am sorry."

"Father" pawed and snorted but she rode him like a cowboy.

What was she sorry about I wondered? I found out seconds later as the centaur galloped towards me. Although I do not remember the moment, I was told I was found trampled, gored and unconscious on the Venetian citadel's summit. Tourists found me the next morning and I was taken to the local dispensary/hospital where my wounds were bound up in a primitive way by the lone doctor on the island.

The chief of police came a few days later with a translator to inform me he could find no evidence of a crime. He grinned when I told him about the centaur. "Even the girl doesn't exist," he said. "No girl ever danced at the bazouki bar. You don't even know her name."

Sebastian had left for Paris so I had no witness.

"You most likely fell over a rock and bleeding fell over another, then had a nightmare as you lay there all night. But what were you up to, out alone that late?" Putting the suspicion on me so he could close his case, I thought, and did not answer him.

As I lay there I had plenty of time to wonder. Do the classical gods exist? They *are* supposed to be timeless. Do nymphs? Griffins? Centaurs? How thin is the veneer of civilization?"

Angelos and I both looked at each other when he paused. Was the story the result of an old man's dementia or could it be true?

"I didn't return to the island for a long time but meanwhile I became known as an artist whose work evokes the legendary creatures of the past. After all I was the only person anyone knew who had actually seen and been wounded by one of them. The girl still haunts me."

"Thank you for listening," the old man said in a courtly way. He arose with the help of his cane and hobbled off. By now the birds were in their roosts, the children in their beds and the waiters were blowing out the candles on other tables as a signal for us to finish up.

"Should we go and see for ourselves if there is a centaur up there?" Angelo said smiling.

"Not tonight," I replied.

DAPHNIS

"Are you familiar with Longus' tale of Daphnis and Chloe?" Angelos asked one June evening while a slow movement of Ravel's ballet of the same name played on the Kastro Bar's stereo. I had arrived on Mykonos just the week before with an extra suitcase filled with art supplies hoping for a productive summer.

"I seem to recall it's a tale of two innocents living *al fresco* in Sicily." I said. Angelos pointed to a man in the corner deep in his cups. "He is a living example of the classical book. Let me explain."

A boy was born whom I shall call Daphnis, the result of a romance between a rich expatriate and a local girl whose favors he bought with gold bangles from Lalaounis, the fancy Athenian jeweler. At that time the natives were quite poor and depended on the sea for their livelihood. Two hundred years before they would have been pirates but now they had traded in their lateen sails and corsair ways for motorized fishing boats.

It was not until after World War II that foreigners discovered the island. The original artists and writers who found a cheap paradise were followed by Greek shipowners and trust fund babies from Europe and America. By the sixties the place was famous. Even Jackie O made an appearance, hence the disco of the same name up the street.

Before Daphnis was born his rich father returned to New York where he went into the advertising business and died of cirrhosis of the liver. When he left because of the very favorable exchange rate the American gave Daphnis' pregnant mother a sum of drachmas decent enough to provide for both her and their child. Of shaky provenance herself, she bought a farmhouse off the road to Panormos Beach, buried her cache in a clay pot, and lived off it for another decade or so. Sale of the jewelry bought another few years. The only income she made was knitting bags and throws for my mother's shop – she had a good sense of the colors, blue, black and white that tourists liked as souvenirs of the Cycladic islands.

Her son grew up haphazardly. He went to the local school

15

– more ambitious students were boarded on the neighboring island of Tinos – but he learned what was important to him from the goatherds who were his neighbors. In exchange for feta cheese and goat milk Daphnis took care of their neighbor's flocks when they attended a wedding on another island or had to appear before the magistrate of the Cyclades in the capital, Syros – a day's sail away.

A near indigent artist from Athens who hand-painted postcards for tourists taught him to play the harmonica, which for both student and artist was the closest modern instrument to the ancient pipes of Pan. By the time he was in his mid-teens, he was both a maestro of the harmonica and a beautiful youth. His mother could not afford a donkey, so Daphnis would run the five miles into town and back again on errands. He was a rose waving in a weed patch. When he was in town, waiting to be paid for his mother's knitted goods at our family's shop, he fingered ancient Greek songs on his harmonica and attracted tourist girls like a pied piper. Being raised by a single mother with no men in the house, he was still a virgin and quite naïve. Women scared him with the sensations they provoked – I know because my background was similar. Life on the islands was old fashioned in those days and I too was raised without a father.

Several years later this changed. He met a strange girl who came out of nowhere while he was sheltering from the midday sun in the shade of a chapel along with his goats. He was playing a tune he had composed himself on his harmonica in the minor Aeolian mode that had its origins in ancient times but can still be heard in rural areas.

"I know that melody," the girl said.

"How could you? I just made it up."

Daphnis stared briefly at the girl and blushed. It was unusual for him to meet someone he did not know. "In Hyperborea it is played all the time when we perform the crane dance," said the girl. She was small and beady-eyed, like a mouse he thought but nice looking, very nice looking. Peeping out of her kerchief he saw a lock of pale brown hair, not usual in these parts.

"Where is Hyperborea?" he asked.

"In the north."

He thought that she was a city person from Athens trying to appear native in her long black dress, and black stockings. The silver sandals with little wings attached she wore gave her away. She slipped away as quietly as she had arrived but promised to return tomorrow.

The next day, Daphnis had feelings he never felt before as he waited for her to show up. He tried to sublimate them by playing so vigorously that his goats began to bleat. Just as they repositioned themselves in the shade raising a cloud of dust, the girl appeared again.

"Where do you live when you're on the island?" Daphnis asked.

"Oh, everywhere. We used to live on Delos but got kicked off."

"No one lives on Delos," he said.

"Yes, we were kicked off."

What a strange person Daphnis thought, but many islanders he knew were also adept at not telling the truth. Some never even admitted their real names, afraid as they were of the evil eye. "My name is Chloe" she said. "*Should I believe her*," he thought.

Chloe gave Daphnis a drink from her bottle. It was pink, cold and delicious and was accompanied by a kiss, then another. Daphnis didn't know what to think.

"Let me show how it's done," Chloe said observing a growing mound in Daphnis' pants.

"Show me what?" Daphnis asked. He was frightened. She proceeded to unbutton his fly and take his untouched penis in her fingers. Deftly she slipped out of her clothes and for the first time Daphnis saw the celestial architecture of the female body. He spontaneously ejaculated. Chloe's nimble fingers raised him again and with legs spread directed him inside her.

It was like discovering the rooms of paradise. The goats paid no special attention as Daphnis and Chloe coupled again twice. When they finished she quickly dressed. "I'll see you tomorrow," she said. Daphnis' eyes tried to follow her path but lost it when she walked behind an oleander bush.

The next day their sex was even more passionate. Daphnis was in in heaven, star struck, as one can only be the first time. For the first time in his life, he uttered those simple words that change history, "I love you."

"If you really do, you must swear fidelity to me. What would you give up for me?"

"Name it."

"O.K. If you look with love at another, you will go blind."

That was nothing, Daphnis said to himself. Young love is immortal – but how many lost lover's names have been tattooed on young skin? Their romance continued through the heat of the summer and Daphnis blossomed nearly into a man. His lovemaking became self-assured. His music came from deeper in his soul.

At the beginning of September, Chloe announced she had to return to her homeland but she would be back next June. "Remember," she said, "you promised me. I stick to my bargains."

Chloe did not return from Hyperborea after the winter. Let me digress about this land the ancients said was beyond the North wind and where Apollo spent the cold months. It was a tradition on classical era Delos that every year two maidens from Hyperborea arrived carrying an offering to Apollo's temple. It is not known what the offering was – only that it was packed in straw. The author Peter Kingsley suggests in *A Story Waiting to Pierce You* that it was a golden arrow, a symbol of the shamans of Mongolia.

But no one has been able to pinpoint exactly where Hyperborea was. In any case the tribute traveled down through the territory of the Scythians who lived in Thrace, the land bridge between Asia and Europe. The Greek historian Herodotus describes how the female guardians and their treasure were handed off like a relay race from place to place in Greece before arriving on the nearby island of Tinos from where they were finally delivered to Delos. According to Herodotus the first maidens arrived in the fabled time when Apollo and Artemis were still resident. Even now you can see the ruins of a small temple on Delos dedicated to the first pair of Hyperborean vestals.

Of course our goatherd knew nothing of this – the mystery for him was solely about Chloe. He pined away as spring progressed. At the same time his muscles thickened as he metamorphosed from a fuzzy cheeked youth to a sturdy young man. The fine point between these two states by the way was the model for the kouros, those masterpieces of archaic Greek art.

Young love is strong, but time can make it fickle. Daphnis became bored with just the company of goats and took to spending afternoons sitting on a seaside rock composing melodies on his harmonica. Beside the rock on either side were two of the best nude beaches on Mykonos, Elia and Agrari. One conjures an image of Daphnis wearing nothing but a straw hat overlooking a multitude of potential muses sunning themselves by the sea.

He learned to speak a rudimentary English when girls from Sweden, France or Austria attempted to pick him up, but he remembered Chloe's injunction. His eyes were not so loyal, as they swept the beach and alighted on one beauty or another. Sometimes this necessitated a plunge into the water to save him embarrassment.

It is said that teenage males know no conscience, and that was surely the case for Daphnis when a particularly attractive dark girl approached who could speak Greek.

"Are you from the island?" she asked him, and said her name was Demetra. Her family came from Andros which happens to be the home island of many ultra-rich shipowners, but Daphnis did not know this.

"I have begun to study ethnomusicology and when I heard the tune you've been playing I recognized something very old," Demetra said.

"I made it up myself."

"Whatever," she replied, and batted her seductive dark eyes. "It would be wonderful for my father and his guests to hear you. He loves the islands and their traditions. Come tonight and play for us. It will be worth your while."

She must mean money, he thought. *She's Greek.* "Where is your home?"

"For the moment we live on that boat." She pointed. Swinging on its anchor a few hundred meters off the shore was a very large white yacht. It had been the source of much beachside speculation when its owners scrunched up on the sand in a Zodiac and sat down to a long-tabled feast on Elia at Yanni's taverna.

Per her promise, a boat arrived at dusk to pick Daphnis up dressed in his peasant best – a rough cotton shirt and black pants. His simple ways and tunes charmed the denizens of the houses of Rothschild, Goulandris, Livanos, and other guests of Petros Ilianos, Demetra's father. Daphnis was their new pet as they drank champagne and nibbled rare caviars.

At the end of his brief performance, Daphnis joined them in a toast to Greek music and found that champagne went down smoothly. After two glasses he was pliable enough to forget his promises to Chloe and be lured into Demetra's cabin. While the other guests sat down to dinner, his loyalty to Chloe was breached.

Sated, his pockets stuffed with drachma notes, Daphnis was returned to the moonlit beach after midnight and walked the dusty weed-lined road home whistling at his good fortune. The contrast was as if he had alighted from heaven. In the morning the yacht was gone.

That day Daphnis dove into the sea at Ftelia Beach. Because the beach was used only rarely for swimming when the infrequent south wind blew - the north wind came on too strong there for all but windsurfers - Daphnis miscalculated the location of a jagged undersea rock. An errant wave thrust his face against its stippled surface. His nose was broken but it healed soon enough – his punctured eyes did not. Local doctors could not save them and now he was like the sightless Homer, or Ray Charles. Blind he could not watch flocks but he still could sing and play mournful island dirges. They fit his new state and delighted tourists eager to hear authentic Cycladic music. He composed new songs with words that echoed his melancholy.

He often wondered if a connection existed between his blindness and Chloe's injunction; also why had she never returned. Once he asked a tourist from the north if Sweden was close to Hyperborea. The man looked at him strangely, then laughed when Daphnis claimed he once met a girl from there. "I'm sorry but she was pulling your leg," he said. Daphnis became a fixture next to Vengera, the chic bar in town. On the other side of the street a friend sold sarongs and changed the coins Daphnis collected into banknotes. Tourists and the Athenians who congregated here were lured by his beauty as well as his music. He was in his early twenties and a source of envy by men for his physique and pity by women for his blindness.

One day some years later a handsome Greek woman whose age could not be determined through the scrim of her make-up and plastic surgery appeared and sat at Vengera for hours. She was moved by Daphnis appearance *and* music. Her name was Afrodite Cannelopoulos and she specialized in eye problems at a clinic she had helped found in Geneva.

"You are an absolute genius to play so beautifully on such an insignificant instrument," she said to him after several days of listening to his songs and observing his sightless charm.

"I don't think it's insignificant. Anyway it's all I have." Some call it coincidence, Carl Jung called it synchronicity, and it may happen no more than once or twice in a lifetime but a life changing turn of fate can occur out-of-the-blue and just when it is needed.

Afrodite befriended Daphnis, offered both to pay for recording his music as well as to attempt an operation she had pioneered to restore his vision, *pro bono* of course, and she promised nothing, but it might work.

It turns out Afrodite could flout destiny and the will of the gods after Daphnis was spirited to the shores of Lake Geneva. An experimental new technique was tried; at first bandages then a blur and the first sight of color since that last blue horizon he had seen as he dived, later focus and for the first time the loving eyes of Afrodite. The operation was successful.

He stayed convalescing in a guest room at Afrodite's lakeside mansion. She invented excuses to inspect his progress, to accompany him to the recording studio, to act as his mentor when business issues came up. She possessed a brittle beauty and manner that his presence made more soulful, she thought. He didn't mean to encourage her. He felt with her the affection that exists between mother and son, so he didn't reject the advances (kisses and hugs) that he knew meant more to her than him.

A fly in this loving milk was Afrodite's teenage daughter – the spawn of a minor German princeling, and Afrodite in her first flush. The girl was athletic, beautiful, and reminded Daphnis of Chloe. His memories of her had begun to blur as his eyesight sharpened and somehow his love transferred itself to a passion for his hostess's daughter. She was named Harmonia after the child of the goddess Afrodite and her lover, Ares. People called her Harmony, a name whose implications (except perhaps for the first syllable) did not suit her. She was willful, sharp to attack and nurse grievances, more like Ares than Afrodite. She could also be charming, intelligent and charismatic and he imagined, an ideal mate for a gentle soul like himself. Initially she resented her mother's obvious affection for this "Greek peasant" as Harmony put it. Later when she saw his cow eyes directed at her, she played up to him to spite her mother.

His melancholy dissipated and he was in love again. The curse of Chloe had played itself out, as he understood it, and he was free of further calamity. Daphnis and Harmony took walks together in the manicured hills overlooking Lake Geneva and picnicked in groves to the tunes of his harmonica. Harmony thought it was ridiculous that anyone would devote himself to such an absurd instrument, but she was between boyfriends.

Her sport was to arrange sex scenarios with Daphnis. Since it was summer most of them happened in the woods and parks around Geneva. The nearly urban locations gave her the extra thrill of possibly being discovered in the act. This provided the "frisson" missing from her lack of attraction to Daphnis.

Like an addict who becomes habituated, she needed more and more danger to satisfy her. When they roamed the woods she took to wearing skirts and no underwear for instant access. Sometimes she would insist they stash their clothes under a tree and stroll like Adam and Eve, ducking behind bushes when a hiker or bird watcher came along. Daphnis had no say in the matter. He was so infatuated that he would do anything short of murder for her. Her brazenness got to the point that on good days they practically lived in the park, swam naked in streams and made love without regard for anyone who might and sometimes did stumble across them. Once a bearded man joined in by masturbating, another time a druggy couple covered with tattoos undressed next to them and tried to form a quartet.

One hazy hot afternoon after he finished a battery of tests to ascertain his progress, Daphnis sat on the veranda attempting to read a Greek newspaper – it had been so long that he had problems deciphering the text. A red sports car careened around the front driveway scattering gravel as it braked. The couple who emerged laughing and holding hands could not see him in the shadow where he sat. Their focus was on each other as they jauntily navigated the corridor that led to Harmony's bedroom. An hour or so later they re-emerged taking a circuitous route via a servant's door down to the driveway and then back in, as if they had just arrived.

"Oh, hello," Harmony said seeing Daphnis for the first time. "You should meet my friend, Dimitri Ilianos." He was a handsome youth of perhaps twenty with the coloring and build that could pass as a younger version of Daphnis. His extreme politeness learned at his prep school Le Rosey was touched with the hint of arrogance that great wealth brings.

"Did I once meet your grandfather, Petros Ilianos?" Daphnis asked. It crossed his mind that he was the right age to be this boy's father.

Their appearance together was like a dagger to his heart. Harmony plunged it deeper into his flesh when, after Dimitri had gone to the men's room, she whispered to Daphnis how much she liked him. "He is a bit naïve but I can teach him a lot. His family owns a fleet of ships and he has been cosseted from the real world. I can be his real world."

"And what about me?" Daphnis blurted out.

"I can take care of you both," she whispered as Dimitri returned and announced he had to leave for an important family dinner.

As you can imagine that evening at his own dinner, Daphnis was a tangle of emotions. On top of it all, Afrodite announced that his operation had been such a success that she had written a paper about it for a conference in America next month. "You'll love it, seeing a new continent and being the center of attention so you must come, too." She smiled at him imagining a situation where they would be alone together. Mentor? Lover?

The following afternoon Harmony was fretting because Dimitri had begged off a rendezvous with her. When she saw Daphnis on the porch she approached and without preamble sat on his lap, put her arms around his neck and kissed him.

"It's too public here" said Daphnis.

"Who cares? Nobody's around" Harmony replied.

Soon they were in the act of half-clothed sex. And to underline that fate can be as unsparing as desire, Afrodite chose just that moment to walk in early from her clinic. At first she pretended not to see them but then doubled back.

"You two little fools," she said and disappeared.

"Mama, I can explain," said Harmony but it fell on deaf ears.

Needless to say, Daphnis' itinerary was changed from America back to Mykonos. Afrodite did not need his physical presence there after all. Harmony ended up marrying Dimitri in a union that lasted just long enough for her to produce an heir that would insure her finances forever. Since Daphnis could never hope to equal his experiences of the lows and highs of life, again, he took to drink. His nature was too complacent to ever ascend to the maturity his age required.

"That's him over there," Angelos said again pointing to the man alone except for his drink who appeared dried up, like a dusty peach or the Duke of Windsor. "Like Aristotle Onassis even at night he wears dark sunglasses. Some say his fragile sight cannot endure the light of reality."

The Last Priest of Isis

After a trying afternoon fruitlessly searching for the right color to symbolize the local Aegean – it can range from an almost black azure through all sorts of blues and turquoises to pale gray, I found myself recuperating at the Kastro bar with my friend Angelos, watching wind surfers in the sea swooping up and down like gulls scavenging food. An American academic, genus WASP, still fit but with white hair and wearing topsiders wandered in and politely asked if the seat next to us was free. After an ouzo or two his Locust Valley lockjaw was loosened enough to tell us about his first visit to Mykonos. His manner was so straight even uptight, there was little question that the strange tale was *not* a fantasy.

My name is Brooks Bowen Brown, a nice alliterative name — I come from an old Boston family. Not long after Groton and Harvard and a year after I published my first short story in *New American Writing*, I decided to spend the summer bicycling the Cycladic islands in the Greek Aegean sea. I was twenty five and if I might brag a bit, in my physical prime – well-muscled from all those afternoons on the squash court and well-informed about life, at least I thought so then, from many mornings in libraries.

I began my tour in Andros cycling through the native island of rich ship owners like the Goulandris and Livanos families, some of whom I knew in school. I toured Tinos, the last island to be ruled by Venice that fell to the Turks in 1715. I paid my respects to the miracle-working icon of the Madonna in its pilgrimage church there and finally crossed to Mykonos on the night ferry. After Mykonos I would wheel myself through Paros, Naxos, Sifnos and as many other islands as I could squeeze in before autumn leaves began to turn in New England.

By now my hair had been bleached from brown to blond from a combination of sun, wind and salt. In contrast to Cape Cod's pale buttocks, my entire body was tan from swimming nude in hidden coves, or on not-so isolated beaches.

I have always been a loner and my social life was spotty. Every two or three days I'd meet a girl who required little prodding to join me in bed and who was free and easy enough to be off again the next morning. Thank god for modern European women. Once in awhile I would meet an interesting character on the road, usually a native, often an eccentric. Conversation was spotty – a mix of gestures and the few words we had in common in English or Greek.

This time was different. It was my third day on Mykonos. On my first I had explored the area around the whitewashed port whose windmills I'd seen on so many travel posters. My second forced me to leave my bicycle in my room – they were not allowed on Delos – the ruined classical city on an island several miles offshore. It was a thrill to see the site of mythical events described by my Latin master Mr. Armstrong back at Groton, like the Sacred Lake where Apollo and Artemis were delivered by Leto as she held onto a palm tree. Now I was circumnavigating Mykonos – not a taxing undertaking, as it is scarcely five miles wide of undulating land scalloped with bays. I wondered why no one cycled here except with motors. It was late in the afternoon when I returned from Kalafati at the eastern and less settled side of the island.As you know, Mykonos is a dry island known for the giant boulders that are strewn over its arid hills, thought to have been deposited there by volcanic explosions, or if you prefer mythology, Zeus, fighting the Titans. However I was bumping through the island's gently sloping and fruited interior plain on a back road. No one was about except one wizened old man in front of a typical white house with a walled garden in back. He was watering geraniums with a curious hose whose bronze nozzle was crafted in the shape of a head of a dragon. I greeted him and asked for some water.

"*Nero*," I said and pointed at my empty plastic bottle.

"Stranger, from where do you hail?" he replied.

It turned out he spoke English perfectly. He batted a hand in the air when I complimented him on his fluency. "My name is Dr. Abaris. I converse in many tongues," he said. After our brief conversation he informed me he was occupied now, but I should return at nightfall to taste his homemade wine. "My vines grow yonder," he said and pointed to a stone fenced green field on the side of the next hill.

I was curious to learn more about this strange old man with his antiquarian English, so I bicycled back as an orange sun that set over the sea behind my back made long shadows. I carried an offering of a boxful of the almond cookies sold on the port. The old man told me to just call him, "Doctor."

I peered around his room looking for medical paraphernalia but saw only an eighteenth century engraving of a figure wearing a long-nosed mask from the *commedia del'arte* entitled "*Il dottore.*"

"Names are unimportant," he said as he uncorked a bottle. "We are known by many names, nicknames, honorifics, etc., etc. in one lifetime. And what about the others?"

"Do you believe in reincarnation?" I asked him.

"It is not a question of belief. It is a fact. Absolutely! Reality."

The Doctor had prepared a small plate of *mezes* – olives, some feta cheese and sliced tomatoes to go with his wine. As we drank, a black curly dog panted in and sat down beside his master. He eyed me warily.

"His name is Argus, after Ulysses' dog. Argus was the only creature to recognize the voyager when he returned from his travels." The doctor patted Argus. "He was once a man, you know. Not a very bright man but nevertheless human. He chose to be a dog because he was disloyal to his friends on the battlefield at Austerlitz. On Napoleon's side he deserted and was killed by a stray mortar shell."

"How do you know the details?" I asked.

"I know. I know," he said and poured me more wine decanted from a faience jug decorated with a blue and yellow classical scene. "Isn't it beautiful?" he asked when he noticed me admiring it. "It is Italian sixteenth century. The rape of Europa – the bull is particularly finely delineated."

The nymph Europa flailing her arms was the last thing I saw as I sank into a deep and drugged sleep.

When I awoke I found myself lying alone in a well-cushioned bed, the sun streaming in. With my eyes still closed, I yawned, stretched and felt the animal satisfaction of simply existing. It took me a moment to realize where I was. I arose and rubbing my eyes peered into an oval mirror that hung precariously by a nail over a marble basin. Only it wasn't a mirror but a portrait of the head of a beautiful nymph. Except it moved when I moved. I blinked. It blinked. I moved my hand to my chest and felt two mounds of flesh. I felt further down where my genitals used to dangle. Now my groin was smooth except for pubic hair surrounding a soft cleft. I took the mirror off the wall and reconnoitered my body. All was perfect tanned skin, curves and folds. I was a beauty, a beautiful girl. In a gesture I'd seen statues of Aphrodite do, I took a towel to cover my breasts and privates and searched the rooms for the Doctor. He was nowhere to be found. In the corner was a still warm pot of coffee, a jar of honey and some bread. In a panic I rustled through his closets but they were empty — even the clothes I'd arrived in were gone. I noticed a gray pleated silk gown lying on a chair with a note pinned to it. "Wear me," it said. I had no choice.

Nightlife is hectic in Mykonos and it did not appear out-of-the-ordinary to see a girl on a bicycle wearing a gown billowing behind in the early morning light. My landlady was up when I arrived and smirked when I asked for my key. I suppose my features as a woman were similar enough to the man I had been for her to hand it over.

"Bella," she said, "Quite a party, eh?" I was sure she thought me a particularly skilled transsexual. That wasn't unique in Mykonos.

I showered and examined myself closely in a full length mirror attached to the door of an armoire. I was indeed a beauty. I would have gone for the person I had become if I were the person I had been. It has to be a dream, I thought and pinched myself. A slight pain convinced me otherwise, something real and strange had happened. I tried to wear what I could of my former male wardrobe. The pants barely stretched over my new hips but a shirt, being oversized, contained my new breasts. When I was dressed I saw that I would have no problem passing for a female.

As I hung the gray-pleated gown in the armoire I found a hidden pocket. In it was a small purse that when opened contained exquisite gold, silver, and copper coins. When I examined them I saw they were ancient Greek – one with the head of Apollo on one side, on the other his lyre; another with Athena shadowed on its reverse by an owl. This cache might be valuable I thought so I hid them inside some rolled-up jeans.

What to do next? Like Lucius, the man who was turned into a donkey in Apulieus' *Golden Ass*, I wondered how I could return to my manhood. At first I was too cowardly to venture forth in public but by sunset I overcame my self-consciousness and stepped outside. The port was at its most heartbreakingly beautiful at that hour. Instead of its daytime blue-black, the sea was composed of tones of gray that subtly interplayed with the reflected white glare off choppy little waves. A departing behemoth of a cruise ship blasted its horn as it turned in the direction of Piraeus – its loudspeakers playing Louis Armstrong. The white walls of town took on golden or blue shades depending on the angle of the sun and its shadow.

As I sashayed down Mykonos' whitewashed lanes I observed that almost everyone male and female noticed my passage. As a straight man, I was used to flirting with women who looked my way, or sizing up my male competition, but never had I been the cynosure of so many hot and heavy stares. A tee-shirted man displaying a torso pumped up from weight lifting tried to pick me up. "I'm not gay," I said to him in a flute-like voice. That had changed too.

31

"You're nuts" he said affronted.

A woman on the next street wearing fishnet stockings and high heels pressed a card in my palm that advertised *Sappho Club – a special place.* "You'd look a lot hotter if you wore high heels," she whispered to me. "I own a shop that sells them."

Why not? I thought. *If this is a dream, I might as well try it all.*

At the shop I had my first girl-to-girl chat with its owner, a tough-looking broad from New York with addictions to fashion and girls. "This butch look has got to go. You could be a stunner. Let me fix you up. Whatever brought you to Mykonos, it was the girls, right? Not exactly Boston, right?"

"I was cycling through the Cyclades," I told her. "I was going to continue on to Paros where a cash transfer is waiting, but now I'm not so sure. I have a collection of old coins I could sell."

The shopkeeper looked at me strangely. "That *is* rich. I'll give you credit until you sell your coins."

An hour later, I tottered out of the shop wearing high heels for the first time. It was fun to be so tall – as a male, now female I was five-ten – the heels added another four inches or so. But it was hell maintaining balance on the uneven streets. The rest of me was encased in clothes to kill – a push-up bra, a skirt that created the illusion of impossibly long legs, a scarf wrapped around that, bangles and gewgaws encircling wrists and neck, and a tiny red purse with almost nothing in it. In short, I looked like a Times Square hooker. Here the code was different. If I thought I was popular before I was even more in demand now. It was so overwhelming that with my few remaining drachmas I bought a souvlaki, went home and cried.

The next day I chose a store that sold high-end watches – Rolex, Cartier, Blancpain – and tried to sell my coins. As I waited for the jeweler's assessment, police arrived, accused me of stealing national treasure and arrested me. Back at the station house they berated me for hours, alternately flirting and leering as they attempted to pry from me the source of my cache. I told them part of the truth. When I mentioned the Doctor, they asked me which one. Of course I couldn't tell them. I described where he lived and they smiled grimly.

"You might be charged with something more serious," one of the policemen said. "The man disappeared yesterday. He is a harmless eccentric, who claims to be the last priest of Isis, over on Delos, but it is not permitted to live there because the whole island is a museum." "I bet those coins came from illegal excavations." I was in a quandary. What could I do? When the police officially confiscated them they asked for my passport. Fortunately the photo of me taken five years earlier was nearly unisex – I looked like a curly headed choirboy then. Since the police had no hard evidence of anything they released me after a long conversation between themselves in Greek but told me not to leave the island. Considering what I had heard, I figured they would sell the coins themselves.

I bicycled out to the scene of my metamorphosis. The house was locked up, and the geraniums were unwatered. I hoisted myself up and peered into the garden. Fig trees, flowers, marble busts and cacti of every variety filled it to overflowing. No one had swept its mosaic-like floor for a long time.

As I returned to town I tried to resign myself to my fate. Lost the urgent desire that used to throb in my pants. No more the hunt. Now I was the hunted. It occurred to me since I had a male brain in a female body I might exploit the situation for all it was worth. If I could ever return, like Lucius the donkey, to my birth body I might as well have experiences denied to my former sex. Meanwhile I could be gay or straight without being gay or straight. What would it feel like to be penetrated? What would two women do in bed? Intimately knowing the male brain, I could lead a man down the proverbial garden path at breakneck speed. I would know which buttons to press to get anything I wanted. More practically I would have to invent a new biography. Fortunately Harvard now admitted women but Groton would be a problem. The name Brooks was unisex but how would I accommodate being an heir of Virginia Woolf instead of Hemingway?

After fixing myself up with a new wardrobe I decided to give my new benefactor a run for her money. I found spending time with her showing me off and allowing a few ostentatious kisses paid my debt. She held me tight as we traipsed from the Sappho Club to a private house dramatically overlooking Mykonos, its dark harbor surrounded by the town like an amphitheatre of sparkling lights. *Heaven for a guy*, I thought as we made our entrance, because there were none. I was introduced to our hostess, a tough-looking Belgian woman of about fifty who I learned by cocktail chatter had made a fortune with hedge funds. She looked me up and down like the proverbial piece of meat. When I was a man, I had been told by women who had swung both ways that females are more romantic, gentle. After being led hand-in-hand to the hostess's bedroom, I had my doubts.

"I reward very well my favorites," she said as she unfastened my bra and felt my curves. In no time we were both naked as she furiously tongued my newly minted private parts.

"You really should shave your pubic hair. It is more chic to have smooth pussies."

I was growing fond of its fleecy texture, like a poodle except softer and I had no intention of doing what she said. When I was male I liked a thatch down there on a woman – it made the region more mysterious. I shuddered several minutes later – my first female orgasm and not so different as I would have thought. But, then I had another one. I pleaded with Ms. Hedgefund to continue, and watched her excitement soar. I knew exactly the right moment to reverse our positions.

"You *are* good," she said when I came back up. She kissed me chastely on my lips then aggressively licked me straight down from my chin, my neck into my cleavage, past my navel and into the lips below. I wondered when my gift would arrive.

I became shameless, exploiting my new body like a toy. I knew what it was like to be a predator as a man – now I wanted to try it as a woman. One day I dressed up like that sensation of 1920's Paris Josephine Baker with a coconut bra and strings of bananas and after midnight went to a gay bar called Pierrot's. I was hailed like Lady Gaga. Everyone wanted to dance with me, everyone bought me drinks, and then they asked me to sing. As a man I could emit little more than a croak. Strobe lights flickered over sweaty bodies as I mouthed words in husky tones, á la Marlene Dietrich, that sent the dancers over the moon. I was a sensation. The owner, Andreas, kept plying me with drinks and slipped banknotes into my bra when I left at dawn with the last revelers. We ended up in another fancy house owned by a gay financial wizard whose boyfriend was Brazilian. By this time the party had degenerated to exhausted men who lay on a large flokati rug in various stages of undress. To be part of the gang I gave a blowjob to the Brazilian who said he craved a woman's touch once a year or so. It was my first. The closest I'd ever come to anything like that before was a circle jerk at Groton. I tried to keep my teeth out of the way as my mouth pistoned back and forth. I was surprised at the turn-on I experienced when I saw I was in control. The Brazilian tried to push his phallus further into my mouth which made me gag. I gently allowed him to feel my teeth and he instantly deflated. "That's not fair," he said and turned his attention to someone else.

The following day I was not such a failure. That afternoon in my frustration at being neither here nor there I determined to be creative, to make happen whatever I wanted. I would take a man in my female guise. I strolled up and down Elia Beach wearing just a sarong and sandals as I scanned oiled bodies basting on towels and beach chairs. I did not care if they were alone or not – I knew that my beauty practically gave me the power of a goddess over a straight young stallion.

On the more clothes optional western end of Elia – the eastern was filled with families shielding their children from physical realities – I espied one particularly handsome hunk, another Brazilian it turned out. His raffia beach umbrella was shared by an attractive girl, naturally good looking and probably lazy because at twenty or so she had no body tone and would shortly show a pooch. Unlike her naked Brazilian she wore a tiny thonged bikini. It was a challenge.

I rented the next chair for fifty drachmas and settled down, flamboyantly unfurling my sarong and displaying my tanned body as I reached up to tie it to my umbrella. Then I walked into the sea in that hip-wiggling way French girls were good at. After splashing around a bit I returned to land, drying my long hair with my head tilted sideways like Aphrodite squeezing out the sea foam. Pretending to grope for a towel and finding none I lay down on my chair glistening and wet. I smiled at the Brazilian who removed his sunglasses, glanced at his girlfriend who appeared to be napping and smiled back. Taking my hint he approached and offered an extra towel, which I accepted. He was smooth. He didn't ask to towel me off or spread suntan lotion on my back or determine where I was from. All I said was thank you, closed my eyes and smiled. I knew he was furiously plotting the next step. As I once read of the 1950's playboy *par excellence*, Porfirio Rubirosa, whose equipment was legendary, this other Latin was likewise spectacularly hung, a condition he aggravated with frequent tugs as he changed positions on his chair. He imagined I had not noticed the squinting eyes beneath his sunglasses.

I went back into the water and he promptly followed. We swam to the rocks that separate Elia from Agrari Beach and here in a secluded cove about as large as a single-bed, we made love without preamble. For the first time I felt what it was like to be skewered. He dripped Coppertone sweat as he pumped in and out. His necklace *figa* charm danced alarmingly next to my eyes and before I knew it I was washing his residue out with saltwater. I wondered if I could become pregnant. "Tell me your name, mysterious lady?" he asked. I remained silent. "When can I see you again?" I remained silent. "That girl I'm with. We are not serious," he said. I remained silent. "You are so beautiful. I am mad for you."

Finally I spoke. "I was a virgin until now. I am a man, you see."

He peered at me first in amazement, then questioning, then in contempt. "You got no balls. You are a loco chick for sure." His face turned beet red.

After he swam back to his monosexual mate, I sat on a rock and contemplated my predicament. It did not feel bad to be the female half of the sexual act, but I liked the male half better. It was what I had grown up with – the thrust, the bursting of the seed, the high albeit brief moment of fulfillment. As a curvaceous woman I was what would have caused my knees to weaken, when I was male but it was not enough.

I contemplated wavelets lapping against the sand in the tiny cove for at least an hour. If I remained female I would spend a lifetime with a disconnect between my body and my mind. As a male again I would know exactly how it feels to be either sex – a great advantage for a writer. I could become the first unisex author, but then wasn't that what all the greats were about. Balzac's *Cousin Bette*, Tolstoy's *Anna Karenina*. I swam back to the sector of the beach where I'd left my sarong and sandals. My erstwhile Brazilian Romeo and his Juliet had gone.

I gathered my possessions and trudged down the beach to my bicycle. Pumping up the hill to Ano Mera and then to the broad valley before town, I found the house where my metamorphosis had taken place. It was locked and dead leaves still covered the floor of its front courtyard. A few palm fronds that waved over the garden wall had turned yellow. I rapped the doorknocker several times, but the only answer came from next door.

"Hello, my dear, what can I do for you?" said a raffish middle-aged Englishman wearing just a scarf around his neck and shorts. He held a paint brush. "Don't stand there in the sun. Come in and have a glass of tea." His paintings stacked around in profusion were abstract but old-fashioned, if that is not an oxymoron – something like Poliakoff if he had been oriented towards Aegean colors – whites, blacks, blues with bright accents of purple, orange and yellow from the local flora.

"Nice work," I said to him.

"You like it?" he said as if he was surprised. "If you're not heading off for an appointment, why don't you stay for an ouzo? I'm not dangerous. You're a beauty but my plumbing shall we say, has clogged. Doesn't affect my eyes, though," he added.

Milky white ouzos soon made our conversation intimate. He told me about his life alone since his wife had died a year before.

"Her name was Persephone, after the goddess of the underworld, you know," he said and laughed. "She was my lifeline to this place, a Greek although not from here. After she left this plane of existence, as Dr. Abaris would put it, I became more of a hermit than I'd been before. But the artist's life is indeed a hermitage." His conversation cruised on and on, like someone truly starving for human contact. I could hardly get a word in edgewise but finally I dropped what I thought was my bombshell.

"You won't believe this but Dr. Abaris turned me into a woman after I had a drink with him. It's not a fantasy either – I used to have a cock but now," I smoothed my hand over the soft curves on my chest, "it's all different." "Oh, I do, I do. You're not the first. I am not surprised. My neighbor has bragged about turning girls into boys, too. Rumors in the village claim he once turned an ass into a dragon to scare off neighbors who were picking his grapes at night. It didn't last long after it ate all the cycads in his garden. He says he is Abaris, the last priest of Isis. "Why would he do that?" I asked. "To check his powers, I suppose, or reorder the universe. You're a young chap. Perhaps he picks the young because they are more malleable than oldsters like me." He leaned forward. "You see that chapel over there. Looks Christian doesn't it? It's not."

A faint light shone from its bottle-glass windows as twilight turned into dusk.

"Dr. Abaris normally worships there every Monday – moon's day, get it? He said when Orthodoxy switched to Sunday, the sunshine burnt out their souls."

"How can I get him to change me back again? Where did he go?"

"Good question. He packed a donkey some days ago – some poor transmigrated soul perhaps, and took off with Argus. Hastily I might add. Before Argus was the guardian of the chapel's door. Now something or someone is in there and my dear I don't want to find out."

"I should try," I said, "There's not much more that could be done to me except return me to my normal gender."

I did try. The chapel I found was unlocked. I opened its door and was illuminated with light halfway between neon and a low-watt bulb. At the altar was the back of a tall robed figure who turned around and temporarily blinded me. Her grayish pleated gown with a knot between the breasts was identical to the one Dr. Abaris had left for me.

"I am Isis," she said. "Kneel, stranger." I felt something whack the back of my knees and I had no choice. "All petitions made to me must come from the position of kneeling." Her voice had a built-in echo. "Do not speak. I have read your fondest wish and I will honor it if you dedicate the rest of your natural life to me. You are a writer. You will write about me."

"May I ask you one question," I said as I gazed around the chamber filled with its magic luminosity.

"I know, it isn't fair. Abaris is a rogue priest – you might have divined he is of the earth. I am of the heavens. You were just his experiment. I have sent him away. If you can prove yourself worthy, you will be my next priest."

My eyes adjusted more to the light and now I could see through the veil of Isis to her face. It was of the most ineffable beauty. I fell in love then and there.

"Do you promise? It is, after all, your fate," Isis said.

"Forever" I replied.

"Tonight around midnight your true body will burst forth like a butterfly."

I backed out bowing and walked over to the artist's house to find my bicycle. "Thank you so much," I said to the Englishman as I wheeled away. "For what?" he replied. The wind swallowed the rest of his words.

I was happy but fearful too. I remembered I had promised the club owner another fling as Chiquita Banana and I needed the money. I was late as I dashed to the club for my 11:30 performance. My fans – by now I had built up a following in the gay community – were restless and ready. I put them over the top with my act, which had evolved to a more complete caricature of Josephine Baker. As the scene became frenzied I plucked the bananas off my costume one by one, peeled and pretended to fellate each one before I threw it into the crowd. By the time I progressed to the final banana and was down to a flesh-colored thong, the dancers went crazy.

This evening it happened differently. Dancing I shed my final banana and suddenly like magic the thong I wore as a woman could not contain me. Having my cock and balls back stimulated me into a full erection. The boys went wild and I felt ecstatic. After I borrowed a towel my employer, Andreas, came over and congratulated me.

"That was spectacular. How did you do it?"

I acted humble, said I had to use the men's room, and inspected what had returned. My male body was none the worse for wear – Isis had even given me a better tan than I had before, and a haircut. All that remained of my female form in the universe were flash photos taken partying. "Who was that girl?" the others in the pictures would ask later. "Remember that night when she disappeared like a supernova?"

"Look at me now, a grizzled husk," Brooks Brown said. "You don't need magic to change your appearance. Time will do it for you." He reached for his handkerchief and blew his nose to camouflage what I felt were tears.

I neglected to ask if he had fulfilled his promise to Isis but somehow knew he hadn't.

THE BEAUTIFUL BOY

"Would you enjoy hearing a sad tale?" I asked Angelos Angelopoulos at the Kastro as we lounged on a quiet June evening, our faces tanned by the last rays of the rosy sun as it fell into a gray sea. On the horizon a bloated white liner cruised towards Piraeus filled with passengers stowing their souvenirs and replaying iPad photos of Petros, the pelican mascot of Mykonos.

"If it won't make me cry" Angelos said and settled back on a cushion like the pasha he claimed as an ancestor on his mother's side.

The other day the appropriately named Diana Nyad tried to swim across the Gulf Stream from the Florida Keys to Cuba. She did not succeed even though at sixty-one years of age she was in top shape. The only reason I mention this not-so-important news item is that it made me remember the would-be naiad I once knew. Her name was Lili. She appeared one day along with her son in a bungalow on Elia Beach. She was a self-proclaimed forty-eight, a former Greek Olympic swimmer and the mother of a sixteen year old, Sebastian.

Lili was not the easiest person to pin down as to facts — who could be who tells you, confidentially, that her father was Nereus, the old man of the sea. She claimed Sebastian's father was English, "out-of-this-world," or maybe Dutch. She spoke in a deep voice she claimed echoed the Delphic oracle. It became even deeper when she was drunk, which she was more often than not. One memorable night someone started a bonfire on the beach. While dancing around it singing off-key melodies, Lili unfastened her bra and tossed it in the flames, announcing nothing could tether her freedom. Rubber in the bra created sparks and stunk up the beach.

Her son Sebastian, on the other hand, was like a male faun — lanky and with the kind of beautiful androgynous face some teenagers are blessed with at sixteen. His skin was as dusky and flawless as the heroes on Attic red figure vases. He was the focus of all eyes, gay and straight — no one knew his sexual predilections, if he had any at that point. His interests lay in local history. He wanted to become an archaeologist.

While his mother Lili swam with her latest inamorata, Sebastian sat in Mattheo's seaside taverna reading and discussing his favorite topics with whoever would listen. Recently he had been to Delos and found a piece of an ivory flute in an excavated wall. He was convinced it was the very one that piped along with the choirs that competed against each other during the ancient Delian games.

Since I too had once wanted to be an archaeologist — after stamp collecting and before Somerset Maugham's short stories became my adolescent passion—we had long discussions about mythical happenings in the neighborhood. Although not very important in antiquity, Mykonos itself had a toehold in mythology. It was here that Hercules helped Zeus fight the Battle of the Titans and buried the last of them under the giant granite boulders that are indeed still strewn about the landscape.

At the time we were all intrigued by the discovery of a bronze age tomb under a mound in the middle of the beach of north-facing Ftelia bay. One day I showed Sebastian a few bits of jet-black obsidian I picked up there — a hint that it was indeed an ancient site since obsidian which was used to make arrowheads and knives is not native to Mykonos but had to be imported from another Cycladic island, Melos. Sebastian had researched coinage from classical times and found out that the few minted in Mykonos were stamped with the head of Dionysus on one side and grape clusters on the reverse. How appropriate even for today when the island fills with charter flight hedonists.

That first summer season Sebastian existed in his mother's outsized shade. During the winter the Aegean naiad and son lived in Holland in Haarlem where Lili had some kind of job importing and exporting flowers and where Sebastian attended school. I did not see them the following summer because, as Sebastian told me, his mother had a new boyfriend and they went instead to Sylt in Germany, the beach resort on the North Sea.

"I hated it but Mother broke up in September so here we are back again."

Two years had helped pop Sebastian out of his cocoon. He was no longer the introvert talking ceaselessly about history and archaeology. Now he was all about style and romance and, to put it bluntly, sex. He stepped out at night wearing the Mykonos look — at that time, gauzy white muslin pants and shirts worn with brightly colored scarves and belts. Around his neck was a gold chain with a figa charm attached (the gift of an admirer, he said) and several bracelets clinked on his tanned wrist. His initial successes attracting glittering eyes increasingly gave him self-confidence. It also helped him realize it was the male gaze that interested him most. I wouldn't call him flamboyant — he was too louche, trying to be too sophisticated for that.

He reminded me of myself when young and I affected a memorable Meledandri suit of tan silk with a white tattersall pattern. A woman on an elevator where I worked then commented that I looked like I had just stepped out of East Egg. I considered it a compliment.

Lili meanwhile had become progressively butch. Her deep voice rasped more. She drank and caroused every night. Although she fiercely assisted and defended her son, they had become two sides of that classical Mykonos coin. He was Dionysus, she was the grapes.

Sebastian began to write poetry, which he shyly showed me and I (not totally honestly) praised. He was obsessed with where his border was in the demarcation of the sexes. He wanted both genders to adore him. His physical attraction to men and a kind of emotional/aesthetic attraction to women (not girls) made him feel split. More than a few of his poems asked why he couldn't be both straight and gay in one body.

45

"Why not a Janus head smiling west
to women staring east to men.
All bodies yearn for love,
why do we have to choose instead"

Adolescent angst, I thought. He yearned to be of noble blood, not one of the herd. This last trait was underlined unpleasantly later when he began to espouse right-wing political philosophy. He was against foreign immigration without thinking through the personal implications. Like Narcissus, he could not pass a mirror without staring. His face had become his talisman. It is a truism that attractive women and men become even more handsome by effort and design because they get used to, and crave the attention their looks engender.

Narcissus's mythological companion, Echo proved to be the aptly named Ekaterina, called Eka for short. She was an athletic and handsome girl of Sebastian's same age who waitressed at Pierrot's, the premier bar at the time. She had escaped from Salonika and an abusive father the year before and came to Mykonos because, considering her circumstances, she didn't much care for men. In fact she thought she might be gay.

When she met Sebastian she decided that she preferred men after all — at least those of Sebastian's less-than-macho type. Fatefully she fell in love with what she couldn't have. Sebastian adored dancing with her and confiding in her but that was as far as it went. He had found out by now there was no better way to attract than to create mystery around his sexual orientation. He became a challenge for either sex. Eka was a wonderful accoutrement — a foil that made him look better.

"Don't you think women are less timid about same sex adventures than men?" Angelos asked. "I've known many who have schoolgirl crushes and gay affairs early. Maybe the impetus of some to have children and thus to need a man overrides their natural bent."

"Not only women" I replied. "Mykonos reminds me that there is no frontier between the sexes, otherwise where would we place the beautiful blonde transsexual I saw tottering on high heels on my way over here."

After a winter's hiatus - Eka in Athens, Sebastian back in school in Holland - Eka convinced Pierrot's owner, Andreas, to hire Sebastian to dance for him. Pierrot's had begun to transition from a bar to a disco — one could charge more for drinks at the latter. To create excitement Andreas initiated a show at midnight to draw in the after-dinner crowd. It consisted of a female torch singer alternating with a beautiful gay boy who danced on the bar. The boy he'd hired the year before had been widely popular — especially when he stripped down to a well-padded thong and several bananas, but that one disappeared onto the yacht of a German prince who would have been King of Bavaria if history had cooperated. Andreas was not immune to Sebastian's charm and he hired him on a trial basis, considering it a minor miracle he had turned up just at the right time.

Sebastian proved to be the best crowd pleaser ever. The shyness of earlier years had vanished and he came alive on stage showing off his delectable body to the primarily gay denizens of the disco that Pierrot's had become. His dancing was sexy enough that eventually he could forego the bananas and just add a gauzy scarf with which to play peek-a-boo. Together with Aretha Franklin amplified to ear piercing thunder he had the audience in the palms of his hands.

When he finished each of his two nightly sets, he was feted by older, rich men who competed to be his sugar daddy. The first of these was a Dutch government minister who said Sebastian was sexier than Donatello's *David*. Why had they never met back home? Who else had he met in Mykonos who could converse in his rare native tongue? He showered him with trinkets — a bangle from Lalaounis, a friendship ring from another jeweler, Kasseris.

Unfortunately when the minister returned to Amsterdam he was never heard from again. Lili, Sebastian's protector in all things, found out he'd gone to trial for misappropriation of money supposed to strengthen dikes along the Zuider Zee. Much fun was made of that in the tabloid press when his dalliances in Mykonos were revealed.

Somewhere down the line Sebastian met an Egyptian singer of about thirty-five who proved to be more significant. He sang in the tradition of Perry Como and Frank Sinatra and was known as the "Crooner of Cairo." His gigs came largely with parties for tourist groups — to make them feel at home. Since few tourists arrived in Egypt in the heat of the summer Moh Al-Kemi as he called himself, could dally in Mykonos spending the foreign currency he'd made in tips.

"Crooner," as Sebastian called him was handsome in an Omar Sharif kind of way — exactly Sebastian's type. Jewelry and other bribes became unimportant for there was a real emotional bond between the two. They discussed whether they'd known each other in previous lives in old Egypt — their attraction was so immediate and intense. Crooner was the father Sebastian never had. Sebastian was the son Crooner might conjure in an incestuous wet dream.

The two became inseparable. At the end of the dancing season, Sebastian returned to Holland with Lili, dropped out of school and flew to Cairo where, as do storks, he was to winter for several years. A complication was Crooner's relatives who would not admit they harbored a gay in the family, an abomination for Islam, and so shunned Sebastian. Sebastian essentially became Crooner's wife, learning Egyptian by shopping for food and watching televised soap operas. He liked his two roles — the yin of domesticity in winter, the yang of being a summertime star.

Eka meanwhile drifted into the lesbian camp. She needed a protector during the off-season and she found several. None lasted. She pretended easy going friendship with Sebastian but what she really felt was a strong love that would not release her. When her mates wondered why she seemed preoccupied, she obfuscated by claiming nostalgia and sadness for her passing youth. This triggered sympathy from her girlfriends and for a while all would be right again.

I lost track of Sebastian for several years, perhaps because my nymph chasing days had elapsed after I had met and lived winters with a ballerina in New York. My annual visits to Mykonos shortened from months to weeks.

The bicentennial of the United States was celebrated in America with fireworks, speeches and reenactments of Revolutionary War battles. In Mykonos we had a lunch party at Mattheo's taverna on Elia Beach. Everyone arrived decorated with some symbol from their hometown. I wore a red apple on a chain around my neck. Piero Aversa, founder of Pierrot's whose former Mykonian lover was its current owner, returned from exile (that is another story) wearing a green rubber Statue of Liberty headdress. Sebastian wore nothing but a diaper to indicate the birth of the next hundred years.

The party began with an attempt to match the otherwise locally unobtainable food for an American picnic — Mykonos lamb sausages for hot dogs, the large beans called *gigandes* for Boston baked beans and corn on the cob. The ersatz American feast was washed down with such copious quantities of wine, ouzo, and Fix beer that by late afternoon the headdress was askew, the apple had been bitten and the diaper discarded. The combination of being high (well, drunk) frolicking in the water, and lying on the baking sand afterward, naked and without a towel made me feel living in one's skin did not get better than this.

When I went back to my beachside bungalow to use the toilet I heard a knock. It was Sebastian who asked if I could help him remove a glob of tar sticking to his foot. I was surprised he had never heard of the easiest technique — douse it with olive oil and it turns to oil. As I toweled off the residue, I practically breathed Sebastian's sexuality.

"I wish you were gay," he said. I've fantasized about it many times since we met. Don't you ever want to try it?"

"You flatter me. I think you're beautiful. I like you but I'm just not that way."

"Just this once" he said. I deflected his entreaties by telling him to put on one of my ballerina's extra sarongs and rejoin the party. He kissed me gently on the lips.

Years passed when I didn't see him. Because of the crowds my visits to Mykonos were increasingly off-season — June and September, while Sebastian was on the island with the Crooner during the peak tourist months of July and August when his dancing was most in demand. On a cold January evening my girlfriend and I were walking briskly along Park Avenue near the Waldorf Astoria hotel when out of a doorway sprang Sebastian.

"Surprise," he said. "I saw you coming." The bigger surprise was seeing Sebastian. He looked wasted. He had lost so much weight that his features were hollow. I embraced him and his formerly spectacular physique felt like bones in a rag bag.

"Are you O.K.?" I asked.

"I've been sick but I'm getting better," he said with no conviction. It looked to me like he had the symptoms I'd been reading about. He told me he was in town for a week with the Crooner who had been commissioned to sing at an exiled Egyptian's fancy wedding.

That summer I heard from Andreas at Pierrot's that Sebastian had died in Cairo several months after our encounter. Talking to Eka who now ran a coffee shop with her girlfriend across from the bar, I found out she had not expunged Sebastian from her emotions.

"He always liked you so much because you took him seriously

when no one else did. But really. It's the same old thing," she said. "We can pretend but we are always alone," Eka said with a theatrical sigh.

"Isn't that the fate of every artist" Angelos observed. "Dancing, especially dancing on bars is so evanescent but like the Italian *commedia* it can be art. Artists have their moments, their stage walk-ons as Shakespeare said, but nothing lasts except the integrity of their art.

"When I think of Sebastian I see the image by Carpaccio of St. Sebastian riddled by arrows. That would be my metaphor-each arrow takes something from the artist's flesh, each work he presents to the world is on its own for better or worse."

I paid my condolences to his mother Lili when I saw her on the port with her new companion an old sailor everyone called "The Captain." The years of drinking had coarsened her and I wasn't sure if she even remembered who I was.

"Those were the days, my friend." Pointing to the Captain she continued, "He missed the wonderful times we had while he steered a stinking tub through the Indian Ocean."

"I have the good times now, my love," he said, with an air kiss, as like a skit from the *commedia del'arte* they caterwauled on down the street.

THE LAST OF THE GHISI

"Yesterday I was reading how Venice played a major role here in centuries past," I said to my friend Angelos one evening at Kastro as we listened to a poignant aria from Donizetti's opera *Caterina Cornaro* (a Venetian herself who was for a time Queen of Cyprus) and stared out to sea.

"I grew up with many Mykonians who claimed they could trace their family ancestry back to Venice," Angelos volunteered.

In one of the synchronicities that seems to happen more than usual on the island who would walk-in but an American friend of Angelos. "Meet Philip Bragadin. He married a Ghisi from one of those old Venetian families," Angelos said.

"I was an artist like you when I arrived," Philip said "but now I manage my late father-in-law's import/export business and try to find time to paint on the side."

"Why don't you stay" Angelos said "join us for a drink and tell your tale. I can assure my friend here it is unlike any he's ever heard."

"My wife Simonetta is off in Ano Mera helping out an aging aunt and won't be back until late. I'll take you up on that drink," Philip said and sat down next to us.

I have always been obsessed with all things Venetian, I must have had another life there. When I was growing up in the Washington D.C. suburbs, I discovered a Dickensian bookshop selling old and rare volumes."

"I collect old books," I said grandly after I negotiated the stairs in a ramshackle Victorian building downtown and rapped on the door. My collection was limited to one eighteenth century French novel that I could not yet read but nevertheless bought the week before for twelve dollars.

The dealer, an Englishman peered at the child of fourteen and to my lasting delight treated me like an adult. "Come in then, let me show you my treasures," he said smiling.

From glass-fronted bookshelves he pulled out wonders, A 1492 Nuremburg Chronicle folio with its famous woodcuts, a musical manuscript by Haydn, a quarto of the neo-Platonic philosopher Plotinus replete with illustrations of the cosmos and printed in Venice over five hundred years ago. I imagined I could actually smell the watery city on its musty pages.

For several years I spent nearly every Saturday in the shop breathing in antiquity. With my meager funds from mowing lawns and babysitting I bought what I could afford – not much. The pride of my collection was a volume of St. Augustine printed in Venice in 1490 with an embossed pigskin binding that I was allowed to pay for in monthly installments. Just fiddling with its brass clasps and tracing its illuminated initials took me back to a time of footpads, doges and argosies to the East.

Following graduation from college and at loose ends I visited Greece for the first time. Someone in Athens told me the Cycladic islands were the place to be so with the flexibility of youth I boarded a ferry in the morning and after eight hours on the sparkling June sea found myself debarking on the last port of call - Mykonos. A bonus that I discovered reading a guide book on my way from Piraeus was that all of them – Syros, Tinos and Mykonos - were once ruled by Venice.

When I was settled I searched out what relics of those days were left. The ruins of a castle on a hilltop near the one inland village of Ano Mera enclosed a chapel in which I found, next to a pinned up magazine page of a Madonna, a memorial stone with a Venetian name, and a roughly sculptured winged lion, an age old symbol of the city. In the port, a row of houses built adjacent to the Aegean as if on a canal is still called Little Venice. Next to it in a square called Alefkandra that contains a perch for the island's mascot, Petros the pelican, two churches jostle for prominence – one Orthodox, the other Catholic. Several tombstones with flowery inscriptions to grandees of the seventeenth century when Venice ruled form part of the tiny cathedral's well-trodden floor.

At that time the island was not as yet overrun by tourists, rich Athenians and seldom used villas of Eastern European oligarchs. Because of a summer art school, would be painters and writers, along with older bohemians in transition, were in residence. Add to this a dollop of expatriates and the denizens of a passing yacht (think Jackie O or Stavros Niarchos) and that was the foreign colony. The natives who were not farmers or fishermen ministered to their needs.

As an artist I was just starting out. Finding a bolt hole in the Aegean where I could spend the summer painting and live more cheaply than in Manhattan was initially brought about by the suggestion of a friend who lived with a Greek girl from Queens. Demi, or more grandly Demetra was a waitress in a bar called Peartree's near Beekman Place where I spent most every evening ending my solitary working days with the reward of a beer or two. "Go to Greece. It will inspire you and if that doesn't help there is always cheap retsina wine," her boyfriend Scott said.

"We met on Mykonos," Demi said in her Greek accent filtered through Astoria. "I had to go there to meet someone from here."

Later Scott told me Demi's father played the zither in a Greek-themed supper club just a block away from the bar. "He isn't too happy about my presence in her life, not being Greek or all," Scott said as he rolled his eyes towards Demi.

Mykonos got into my blood quickly. I loved the sere hills smelling of oregano, the constant wind-blown sunshine, and the indigo seas that framed the island. Whitewash extending even onto the streets gave the jumbled town's architecture a cubist unity; the purples and reds of bougainvillea, deep blues of morning glories and pinks of oleanders provided its accents. Anyone seen against a white wall became an instant Avedon photograph.

When I first espied the young woman who would become my Laura, my Beatrice, she sported a kind of turban affixed with little gold coins that covered her hair and a long crimson robe cinched with a yellow and green checkered belt. Her eyes were as gray as Athena's, a feature that made her stand out from the usual black or brown stares of the locals. She glided by me quickly in the maze of streets behind the harbor one evening and again a week later. She made an indelible impression – perhaps it was her complexion, which was paler than anyone else in town, nearly like a ghost. And she was beautiful.

Those piercing gray eyes haunted me and I began to look for their owner. Every evening I trolled the back lanes where I had seen her and explored the neighborhoods from where she might have come. It took another week but I hit pay dirt on the evening of St. John's Day, June twenty-fourth, when wreaths woven and dried since Easter are burned in little piles on the street. It is a quaint custom with an origin in antiquity, whose purpose is to bring good luck for the following year. The pale one was in a knot of people observing young girls jumping over the gathering flames. I watched for a minute or so before she caught my eye. With her fixed and spare smile in the twilight she reminded me of the Mona Lisa.

When the group broke up I skulked after her until she entered a door opposite Maria's Garden, a restaurant in the middle of the labyrinth of Mykonos. For the next several days it became an obsession to pass by that door as often as I could. It had no identification other than a corroded iron doorknocker in the shape of a winged lion. I considered rapping on it pretending I was looking for someone, but didn't have the nerve to contemplate what I would do next.

Finally one day after a lunch in the port at Antonini's taverna, I traversed again what was becoming a well-worn path. Ahead of me walked a local character – a white-suited old man I'd seen selling nuts on the waterfront that he scooped out of a curious glass and tin container. He turned and slipped through the door guarded by its winged beast. I managed to glimpse a courtyard with a clothesline and some geraniums planted in rusty olive oil tins. Was he her father, grandfather, or just another tenant in the whitewashed warren?

That evening as I sat with my pre-prandial ouzo at a café on the harbor I beckoned over the old man wearing his signature fisherman's cap. In the process of buying a small paper bag of pistachios, I considered asking him about the girl who appeared to live where he did but couldn't think of a way to approach the subject without sounding as if I had been following her. In any case, in my pursuit of the pistachios' price I realized his English was non-existent – he just pointed and picked out the coins proffered on my outstretched palm.

Good luck arrived the next day. On a back street near the store that sold foreign newspapers was the tiny gallery of a black-bearded artist who sat and painted icons in the rear of his narrow space. I had never entered the shop – I knew I couldn't afford his wares even though I felt a strong affinity for the icons he displayed in the windows – but I had peered into the gloom and imagined he must work with the help of light reflected from the icons' gold backgrounds. This time I saw the gray eyed one rearranging pamphlets. This time I stepped in.

She glanced up at me with a vague smile and said, "*Kalimera.*"

In response I blushed but, standing against the light, hoped she would not notice. "Very nice. *Oraia,*" I said, pointing my finger at a wall of images. The artist looked up to acknowledge my presence with a nod but went quickly back to work using an old-fashioned palette locked in his thumb and a mahl stick to direct and cushion his painting hand. The girl stood demurely, her hands coupled in front and followed my glances at the art. As I pretended to look, I was roiling inside. How could I approach this creature whose presence made me tongue-tied.

"Do you work here?" I asked. How lame I thought, but she answered. "Yes."

"I see you speak English," I replied.

"School," she said and pointed at her lips.

How could I unlock our laconic exchange? "I am an artist, too, a painter. I've been influenced by icons. I like Byzantine art." This elicited a spark in her gray eyes. "I don't paint religious subjects, though. Mine are pagan. Based on the myths," I added.

"Oh, myths," she replied, as if it were something new to consider.

"Would you allow me to buy you a coffee on the port? We could discuss art," I blurted out. My heart raced until she answered.

"Maybe," she said with her head down, "but I cannot leave the shop. Maybe at eight thirty, I can go."

"Wonderful," I said, relieved. "By the way, I don't even know your name."

"Simonetta," she said.

"That's not Greek, is it?"

"Venetian," she said. "My family is from Venice. Even though we have lived on Mykonos for many centuries." This was a concept Americans like me could not fully understand.

We continued our conversation at a café that evening. I did most of the talking – she was not so much shy as inscrutable, like a sybil might be – taking it all in so she could pronounce a riddle on my fate later.

"I like icons. That's why I entered your shop. I like their presence." I wondered if she understood what I meant. "But I don't understand the tradition of endlessly copying originals supposedly painted by St. Luke." Simonetta just looked at me which made me nervously continue. "I prefer to introduce an image into the world that's never been seen before. Like Carpaccio's St. Ursula in bed."

"Who is Carpaccio?" she said breaking her silence.

"One of your greatest Venetian artists."

"Ah," she said.

"I have never been to Venice," she said, "but I have seen photographs and I have imagined it. I grew up hearing tales of *La Serenissima* from my father who heard them from his grandfather. We used to rule these islands, you know."

It reminded me of my junior year of college in Paris where I boarded with an exiled White Russian family in Passy. They would argue at the table who had the noblest blood. "*Bonjour mon oncle,*" the man would say when we passed the equestrian statue of his uncle *Pierre Premier de Serbie* in the nearby square named after the king. His wife, a princess from Russian Georgia, read books about antebellum plantations that reminded her of home. I felt that I was cheated in this lifetime, being born into that epitome of the 1950s, an American middleclass family. I fancied myself more – perhaps that is why I became an artist.

In any case, our coffee went well and my proposal to see Simonetta over dinner the next day was accepted. Not only was I enraptured by her physical beauty (what I could see, at least – her face and hands), but I found her demeanor quaintly charming. Unlike other women of twenty-two in the modern world, she apparently had not been much affected by it. Venice still had a chance to become a republic again and re-establish itself in the archipelago. Icons were a direct route to God. Pirates might be corsairing somewhere beyond the horizon. She believed in the sanctity of marriage and keeping her virginity, etc. Her very unavailability made me all the more infatuated.

After dinner I tried to hold Simonetta's hand as we walked back to her door, but she would not allow me. "It looks bad," was all she would say. During the next dinner, pretending to drop my napkin I did manage to brush her hand under the table. She grasped mine for several seconds before placing hers back in her lap. I could tell she liked me. Some of the distance I'd first encountered had faded away and a warmth had spread underneath her pale skin. I asked her why, unlike most everyone else on the island, she didn't sunbathe or swim. She claimed it was not ladylike.

"But it feels good," I said.

"Many things feel good. That doesn't mean they are good. It would feel good to sleep after daybreak in summer but it is not permitted."

Thus it was a total surprise when the next day at a pre-arranged date for ice cream and peaches at a waterfront café, she proposed that I meet her parents. "My father would like to talk to a fellow Venetian," Simonetta said. "I told him what you said last night, that you might have ancestors from Venice on your father's side."

"It's only a small part of me – one grandparent."

"That's enough for him. There are few Venetians here with even that much."

The evening of the dinner arrived and I presented myself at Simonetta's door promptly at eight with a box of the almond cookies sold to tourists as an island specialty. A hunchbacked crone dressed all in black smiled a toothless grin as she swept me in. I felt like Little Red Riding Hood being ushered into the wolf's lair before Simonetta appeared, all bubbly with none of her usual guardedness and accompanied me into the next room. While we waited for her father to appear, I took in its tarnished mirrors, foxed engravings, a dusty Venetian glass chandelier and a case of mouldering leather volumes. As I read their gold stamped titles – Pitton de Tournefort's *Journey to the Archipelago,* George Wheeler's *Travels in Greece*—I was interrupted by the sudden appearance of Papa—entering *con brio* in a satin smoking jacket, once black but now greenish on the edges. His brilliantined hair was swept back, too black to be natural. With a thin moustache à la David Niven, he looked like a parlor snake from an old movie. "Alvise Ghisi," he said, and shook my hand.

He was cordial, inquiring about my journey as if he imagined I had just arrived from overseas. "How goes it in Venice?" he asked. Not wishing to disappoint him, I replied that except for too many tourists and more frequent *aqua alta*, I guessed all was pretty much the same. I did not say that I had never been there.

The crone turned out to be Simonetta's aunt and the wife of the nut man when we sat down to dinner. Simonetta's mother, who appeared soon after carrying a large serving bowl of fish soup, wiped her bejeweled hands on an apron before being introduced She was more elegant than the aunt, but also wore black.

"It is one of the joys in life that my wife makes the best *bouillabaisse*," said Papa as he raised his glass of wine. "All the fishes are from local waters," There was little conversation as we dug in, spooning up the soup and prying small bits of edible fish from among a thicket of bones. The next course, chewy goat meat, was not much easier in the able-to-eat department. Simonetta kept glancing over at me, then at her father, as if to ascertain his level of approval or mine. Finally, *loukamades* appeared (fried, sugary doughnuts), along with glasses of a sweet wine. "From Monemvasia, in the Morea" Papa said, "a stronghold for us like Gibraltar." The Morea was what Venetians used to call the Peloponnesus. Monemvasia, I knew, was a big fortified rock. "Have you ever graced those shores?" Papa asked me.

"My knowledge of Greece is limited to Mykonos and a brief stay in Athens, I'm afraid."

"No matter," he replied. "Do you know that Tinos over there was the last Venetian island to fall to the infidels. In 1715," he said, and pointed out the window to a view of the adjacent island now just a dark blot on the horizon except for its port's twinkling lights.

The women repaired to the kitchen and left the men at the table growing mellow with fresh draughts of the amber wine and with the cigars Papa passed around. "My hobby," Alvise said, "is the history of the years Venice was dominant in these parts, beginning with Marco Sanudo in the thirteenth century who became Duke of the Cyclades. It is thought by some that my family is related."

On a ledge, he pointed out some of his treasures – one was a glass faced box holding a wisp of reddish hair. "The very beard of Barbarossa," Alvise said. "I found it in the bazaar in Istanbul." Barbarossa, as it happened, was the quasi-pirate captain working for the Turks who terrorized and plundered Mykonos in the sixteenth century. "And this is a rare Mykonian coin from the classical period. He lovingly fingered the nearly indecipherable bronze coin as he held it up to the light.

"But enough of dead relics. Tell me more of your own Venetian heritage. Your surname, I'm told, is Bragadin. You can make no mistake of that. You must be related to the heroic admiral who was flayed alive because he would not surrender Famagusta in Crete to the perfidious Ottomans."

"My Italian grandfather died when I was very young. He had little chance to go over family history."

"He must have been adventurous to travel to America."

"I imagine his reasons to emigrate had more to do with economics.

"Ah, so he was a trader. That is my background too. I buy and sell towels and sheets and fishnets."

"Not exactly," I said, and decided to end it there. He poured more sweet wine and my head began to feel a bit woozy. It cleared up quickly when he spoke again.

"This is a matter of some delicacy but I want to propose something that has to do with my beloved child. She has reached her majority but there is no one with noble Venetian blood on Mykonos for her to marry. The few that were here left some years ago to become seamen or establish (I believe you call them) short-order restaurants. I have no sons to continue my family business, so Simonetta's dowry might be substantial."

What an invitation! I was infatuated with his daughter, but the prospect of spending a life flogging nets to local fishermen, sheets to their wives, and towels to tourists would be a death sentence. "Sir, I am an artist. It is a calling I could not easily give up."

"Be that as it may, I have a good staff who are accustomed to doing the work of the business. Surely you would have time to supervise – in between painting, of course."

I glanced over at Simonetta. How much of this proposal was her idea, I wondered?

"Think about it, young man. I feel I can trust you – we all had to trust each other when we put together our annual argosies to the East. It is a trait that has helped us Venetians survive all these years."

Simonetta smiled when, if only to break away, I told her father I would think about it. She led me to the door, holding my hand tightly, and placed a firm kiss on my cheek before opening it.

"I hope my father didn't scare you."

Have you ever found yourself at a moment when one's destiny meets a fork on the road? On the one side was freedom to follow my art wherever it led; on the other, the love of a beautiful woman laden with familial obligations. I had been infatuated many times before. If I chose Simonetta how could I be sure this time it would last? I didn't feel ready to make such a life-altering choice.

The next evening we took in a movie in the open air cinema. It was in garish Technicolor, and had been initially released several generations before in Hollywood. Called *The Black Robe*, it was like a shoot-em-up Western but took place during the Crusades. In several lengthy breaks caused when the celluloid broke, Simonetta and I flirted and ate ice cream while inwardly I agonized over the decision I was being forced to make. Simonetta seemed more beautiful than ever. I tried to massage her rigid back.

"Relax," I said.

She turned and flashed a big smile that melted me, but continued to sit primly and upright. "Some of these people are neighbors," she said.

Simonetta did not make things any easier when I walked her home through the maze of the town smelling of chalky whitewash and night blooming jasmine. A full moon rode overhead – it was a night for romance. When I kissed her goodbye she pulled me into the outdoor foyer, pressed her body against mine, and allowed me for the first time to fondle her breasts through her dress. While we kissed I went the next step and rubbed my body against hers, hoping she would feel my urgency. This caused her to abruptly break away. "Tomorrow," she said as she hurried inside.

"My father asked me to find out which way you might be leaning. Without forcing you, of course," Simonetta added. She did not look at me but gazed out to sea, watching a ferry from Porto Rafina let down its anchor chain with a great clatter off shore as we sat together at a café on the waterfront.

"You know my feeling for you, but these things don't happen overnight. In your father's mind, I feel our future is a business transaction which only needs a handshake to go forward."

Simonetta continued to stare pensively at the harbor's activity – lighters shuttled passengers to shore over water too choppy for the ferry to dock.

"Would it make a difference if I gave you everything?" she said.

"What is everything?" I asked, knowing full well what she meant. The Victorian age was propositioning the twentieth century. Virginity, the great prize then was now a detriment. I felt a fresh burst of loving emotion for Simonetta. She was so naïve. She needed a protector. That man I doubted was me.

Later, after accompanying Simonetta on the *passagiatta* by the harbor side, we ended up scaling the slight bluff atop which Mykonos' signature windmills stood dark and silhouetted against a starry sky. We found a quiet, hidden spot where we could kiss. As eighteenth century novelists would have it, Simonetta's defenses began to waver, then fell.

"Take me so I will remain a virgin," she said. It was so uncharacteristic of what had happened before with Simonetta that I hardly could believe it.

"Are you sure?" I asked.

"I have made up my mind," she said. Both of us partially disrobed. She guided me in and a stronger love than I'd ever felt mingled with desire and lust, made me come too quickly. Afterwards, we kissed for an hour under the clacking of a windmill's vanes propelled by a brisk wind.

That night it was difficult to sleep. Making love had resolved nothing for me even though I imagined it meant everything to Simonetta. What I really needed was a girlfriend willing to treat living together as an experiment with no further strings unless things became "serious." What she seemed to prefer was a tightly-laced corset of rules and obligations. With the hubris that I could manage to finesse the ways of an ancient civilization, I decided to string out the status quo as long as possible. A formal lunch followed with her parents politely avoiding pushing me (I felt) into a decision, but seeming anxious nevertheless. They smiled benevolently when I asked if it was customary here to ask the father for his daughter's hand in marriage.

"Of course, old boy, it is, but I think you know what my answer would be."

The next few evenings, Simonetta and I coupled under a eucalyptus tree in an abandoned courtyard, lying in a fisherman's boat bobbing at anchor in a desolate cove, and, most dangerously, in a gardening shed attached to her own house. Each time my love for her increased and I was sure it was reciprocated. Each time it was the same odd maneuver to maintain her virginity. The as-yet unattained goal made me all the more amorous.

It also directed me to a jeweler where I bought a simple ring with a tiny diamond embedded in it and presented it to Simonetta over a sundown drink (tequila sunrise) at the Kastro Bar. She was thrilled, of course, shed one of her inhibitions, and kissed me publicly to the accompaniment of a Maria Callas aria from *Tosca*.

"We have to go and tell my parents," she said as she admired the hand that wore my troth.

When we saw them they congratulated us both, smiled a lot, wiped off cobwebs and uncorked a bottle of champagne long resident in the cellar waiting for just such an occasion. Still, I sensed something troubling behind all the *bonhomie*.

"Have you told him yet?" I heard her father say to Simonetta. She shook her head.

"Later, Papa, later."

What could it possibly be? I wondered. An issue about her dowry? During a festive supper afterwards we held hands openly and I was even encouraged by the nut selling uncle to kiss Simonetta to general gaiety.

When we were finally alone together, sitting on a terrace that was actually the roof of a neighboring house, I asked Simonetta if something was bothering her.

"Not really. Isn't my love enough?"

"If there is something, you should tell me now. I've always considered myself a wanderer. I'm taking a big leap connecting myself through you to a specific place in the world," I said, immediately regretting that my words came out sounding like a prig.

"You paint imagined paradises. Even those of Mykonos are fanciful versions of the real thing. Perhaps it will be good for you to anchor yourself to me and my island."

My doubts were largely assuaged in the following days as in-between discussions of wedding details to be performed in the Catholic cathedral, we were carried away by the constant lovesick hugs and honeyed words all new lovers embrace.

Finally one evening I could stand it no longer. As a result of constant pleas, Simonetta agreed to arrange a subterfuge so she could spend the night in my room. She told her parents she would overnight at the home of one of her school friends (and bridesmaid) to discuss her wedding dress.

After a pre-arranged rendezvous near the bus stop that normally would transport her to the village of Ano Mera and her friend some five miles distant, she wrapped her arm around my waist and we walked on the least-frequented lanes to my room at the Hotel Matina. The hotel was set in its own garden and fragrant aromas of night blooming flowers wafted up to the small balcony where we sat and talked quietly of our future. By now I had come to terms with abandoning my total focus on a career as an artist. I would, in effect, pander for a while to Simonetta's father – we both agreed that would give us security early in our marriage. And afterwards, who knows? We could live the warm parts of the year here and winter in New York. She was already thrilled with the idea of residing off the island at least for a time. As to children, "the two of us will be enough," she said, while her father had once mentioned grandly that he might be the last of his line, that it would make him akin to the last doge of Venice or Louis XVI. "All things crumble," he said in one of his reflective moods. All he wanted out of life was for his only child to be happy.

For the first time I would see the object of my desire without barriers – naked to my gaze. Her shyness as she disrobed brought a pang to my heart – maybe there was something after all to the old tradition of presenting virginity to the man you would marry. She insisted on darkness as, with her back to me, she folded her clothes on a chair and slipped under the sheet. In the dim light beaming from the moon, I saw that Simonetta trembled as she lay there. I remembered how nervous I had been the first time when my high school girlfriend and I were both deflowered on the rec room floor after my parents had gone to bed.

Slowly, like a butterfly, I brushed my lips against hers. Slowly I pulled down the sheet to reveal her perfect breasts. I sucked on them until her nipples stood out like pencil erasers. Further down I felt her washboard ribs and tongued her navel. Finally I reached the edge of her pubic hair, black as coal in the moonlight. I pulled off the sheet and received the surprise of my life. An erect penis lay there in its dark nest which Simonetta swiftly covered with her hand. I could do nothing but stare in disbelief. Was it some kind of joke? I removed her hand and reached out to touch it. Indeed it was real and throbbing. I could find no words to express my emotions, as mixed up as the circumstance. Simonetta began to cry.

"I wanted to tell you but I fell in love and I did not want to ruin it. You made me know what love is." My heart went out to this pathetic creature whose erection by now, like mine, had wilted away. What were my emotions? Had I been in love with a fantasy?

"Does your family know?" I blurted out before realizing how stupid that sounded.

"Yes," she said. "Since I was made on the cusp between male and female, my family knew I had to make a choice. I couldn't have children but it was more practical to be seen as a woman. Plus Papa always wanted a daughter. I was born with the help of a midwife from Tinos who they paid off to keep the secret. It was easier to hide my privates than the breasts I eventually grew and as a girl, I was not subject to national service. Papa was not altogether surprised – every other generation or so someone like me has arrived in our family. It was even considered a blessing because each time one of us appeared, our family prospered."

I did not know what to do. A thousand thoughts darted through my mind as I lay there cuddling her naked body. I too shed some tears for the unfairness of it all.

Just after dawn the next morning, Simonetta slipped out of my room and made her way back home. In her absence, like an earthquake or a revolution, I felt the physical facts of existence rearranging themselves. It was a surprise my emotions did not – I was as much in love with her as before. The question I mulled over all day was whether I could spend my life under the newly revealed circumstances.

When I saw her that evening at our pre-arranged café rendezvous, when I felt like a mosquito drawn to the flame of her radiant smile, I knew that whatever we had between us was stronger than sex or gender.

"I guess you will always be my girl," I said as I took her hand and played with the finger that held her engagement band. Simonetta said nothing but in the immortal language of lovers, placed her head softly on my shoulder as we watched the wide variety of human beings promenading by us on a sultry August evening on the formerly Venetian island.

"So that's my story," Philip said. "Some things in life happen not merely as a surprise but as a reordering of the universe."

Angelos and I nodded. Our loves had been prosaic in comparison.

"Could you accept a skewing of your natural proclivities with a discovery like that?" I asked Angelos after Philip had left.

"What a fancy way to ask if I have a gay streak," Angelos said.

"I've read that each of us sexually is somewhere on a continuum between gay and straight. Perhaps Philip's love for Simonetta just pushed him a little further left on the scale."

"The question is," said Angelos after he ordered another ouzo, "where on the scale is Simonetta?"

RETURN OF APOLLO

"Back in the days I wasn't the only artist living out here in one of the bungalows" I observed as we sat at Yanni's taverna watching the six o'clock rout of sunbathers from Elia Beach.

"You mean the painter with the unfortunate name – Nick Eclipse?" By coincidence Angelos had just recently found out what had happened to him.

"I heard from a mutual friend that Eclipse was arrested some years ago for seducing a thirteen year old girl and spent time in jail. In the Big House he turned from painting to writing and sent a story to my friend who edits an obscure literary magazine. Eclipse told my friend it was a memoir and "as true as can be!" In light of some recent best-selling 'memoirs' that have proven to be fiction, my friend wanted to know if I could verify the events described and sent me a copy. I told him Eclipse did indeed have a dicey reputation and events might have occurred in the way he remembered, but I knew nothing definite." "I still have the copy. If you read it perhaps you could add something."

Return of Apollo by Nicholas Eclipse

To pay for my initial summer on the Greek island of Mykonos (when I first took the plunge as a full-time artist) I worked half the day painting small works I could later sell for cash to a gallery in Germany. The other half I spent studying anatomy on its nude beaches.

As I discovered one wine-soaked summer afternoon when the art dealer took me to meet some of his fellow barons and counts (and drum up customers for an upcoming exhibition), they all lived in castles surrounded by vineyards along the Moselle and Neckar rivers whose slopes produce some of Germany's best rieslings.

"You can see, their walls are already covered with antlers and old masters with generous attributions," Graf Von Knyphausen said. "They will only buy small canvases. That's all the wall space they have left, but they will buy because each generation wants to leave its mark."

He encouraged me to paint snowy scenes in browns and grays, preferably with hunters and scudding clouds illuminated by moonlight – nothing too colorful. In the course of several shows at his castle I hollowed out a little career akin to those seventeenth century genre painters in Holland who specialized, for example, in painting variations on the theme of sailing ships in windswept seas. I knew that "going commercial" as my friends called it was a diversion from my truest talents but it was better than stapling up dry walls back home. To save money he let me stay in his own small curio-filled castle, nestled in a romantic park filled with meandering gravel paths and nineteenth century monuments to illustrious ancestors and their exploits in forgotten wars. Here I met worthies from the Stuttgart region who were his friends, one a former mayor and son of the desert fox Field Marshal Rommel; another, who spoke beautiful Victorian English I was told later would have been the Kaiser.

In Mykonos I rented a tiny room, locally called a bungalow, on the beach at Elia five miles from town. At that time it was inaccessible except by boat unless one's innards could stand a rutted road little more than a donkey path, and if one could find a taxi that would reluctantly take you there. Beside my bungalow there were just nine others, and two small tavernas. After eight at night when the electric generator was turned off, it was a cove outside of time. Like my paintings, it was a small existence but had its compensations.

One day among the beach blankets and tanning bodies, the most beautiful man I'd ever seen strolled by. I'm not gay, but I could see the attraction of his jaunty manner, his toned physique, his crown of golden curls, even the small harp slung over a shoulder that looked right at home on him. He fit in no category – not a student, a hippy, an artist, writer, or a slumming businessman. By the evidence of his instrument I guess you could call him a bard, and I discovered later that he did indeed strum it to accompany tunes and words he claimed to have invented. I did not approach him at first but heard from acquaintances that his name was Paul Delphinius, that he came from Munich, and that he was neither straight nor gay but both.

Until he arrived the nymphs from Scandinavian countries with creamy white skin that needed high-numbered protection lotion used to be my province. After gently sliding my hands over the ridges of their spines and "inadvertently" massaging the sides of their breasts or a bit into the cleft of their upturned buttocks, I might suggest lunch and then a nap in my bungalow. Now they sat around the German as he regaled them with stories, jokes, and even went so far as to pretend to read their palms. What did they see in him?

I found myself setting up my beach towel close enough for me to observe the goings on from behind sunglasses and try to figure him out. I wondered where he lived – not in the bungalows, for sure, and he never seemed to require transportation. He just walked onto the beach every day from parts unknown and unfurled his tacky beach throw – actually a large towel I'd seen for sale at a shop in town that featured the words "*Mykonos/ Delos, Birthplace of the Sun.*" I suppose it would have some charm back in cloudy Bavaria. Out of his back pack invariably came a golden-colored Frisbee – Helios he called it – which he would throw to whatever partner he could rustle up.

If you can't beat 'em, join 'em, I decided when my personal famine stretched out for days. This was not what I'd come to Elysium for – I could do better finding willing girls on a Manhattan subway at rush hour.

"Hi," I said in my breeziest, friendliest manner as I walked over to Paul's towel surrounded by his bevy of adoring naked nymphs. It didn't help that I tripped over the sexily outstretched limb of one of them as I approached. They all laughed. "I hear you playing your harp sometimes. I'm an artist, too, of the visual category. Name is Nick Eclipse. From America." How fatuous I sounded. "Welcome to Mykonos," I added, as if I owned the place. Fortunately Paul (if not the girls) extended his hand to join him in his radiant circle.

"By the way it's a lyre not a harp" Paul said correcting me. "What an unusual name. Where does it come from?" he asked.

"Family lore says we are Czech, related to Copernicus. And you are from Munich?"

"Not originally. Actually, my family comes from around here. I've returned to my birthplace, you might say." The girls tinkled appreciatively for no reason. *What a lot of guff*, I *thought*. "And what are *you* doing here?" Paul asked in a mocking tone as if I was trespassing on his territory.

"It's a great place to paint, it's cheap, and there's a lot to look at," I said sweeping my arm over his knot of admirers and fastening my gaze on one particularly fine and pendulous breast.

"Isn't it fantastic not to be belted and zippered into cloth?" Paul said. Had he noticed my stare? "In Munchen we have the *Englisher Garten* where we can go naked in the middle of town. I've written a song about it." He picked up his lyre and proceeded to strum along with a short ditty. "That's in ancient Greek," he said.

How pretentious, I thought. "Are all your songs in a dead language?" I asked with a challenge in my voice I hoped would resonate with his entourage.

"It's still living," he said, "if I use it," and then translated the words into English – something about overall tans on frolicking maidens. He continued on with another verse as my ogling eyes swept over his band of admirers, all of them female except for one boy – seventeen or so with exquisite golden locks and lithe limbs, like a smaller, more precious version of Paul. *He must be gay*, I thought, the way he ignores the girls and stares at the Elia minstrel with a Mona Lisa-like smile. I found out later the boy's name was an ancient Greek one, Hyacinthus – so-called after a favorite of Apollo. His parents were classical scholars and archaeologists in Athens who should have known better. The mythical Hyacinthus was accidentally killed by a discus. In any case, we called him Hy.

As I examined Hy, I began to tick off reasons ancient Greek men could fall in love with young guys. Adolescent boys embody the good side of free and easy sex without the hang-ups that come with girls. Keeping one's virginity for marriage, messy menstruation, and the sheer flibberty-gibbet quality of teenage cock teasers – all can be avoided. My stare drew Hy's attention for a moment but he turned back to his adoration of the minstrel while adjusting his equipment.

I decided Hy was not altogether gay when he placed his golden flecked arm tenderly around the slim girlish shoulders of one of the semi-circle of nymphs. Her name I knew was Daphne because I had flirted with her before Paul arrived on the scene – she also was about seventeen and ripe for the pluck in my opinion. Although her father was Greek, her mother was English. In my experience, English girls were the raunchiest of all. Daphne's raptness seemed more for the quaint song than its strummer as she flicked her lashes at Hy and cuddled in closer. The beach girls come and go on their charter flights and I had slept with none of these recent arrivals. All of them so golden and beautiful – the world before them and me showing the first sag of age. I could already pinch an inch or two at my waist.

Paul began a rap now in English with a strong German accent about a dark artist who came out at night, who could see only by moonlight, whose color sense was all about silver gray and dark shadows. It took several stanzas to recognize he was mocking me – several more for the others to get it, turn towards me, and smile. Of course I smiled, too (sticks and stones, etc.), but I felt my grin was like that of a skeleton's skull. How could Paul know about my work? I'd told him nothing; his admirers knew nothing, either.

Daphne, I gathered, was too naïve to understand Paul's mockery of me. "Could I see your paintings sometime? I love moonlight," she asked sweetly. A swell of vindication added to my certainty that I could isolate her from the herd.

"It would be more than charming if you would come to my bungalow," I replied.

That very afternoon she knocked but unfortunately brought Hy along. Fortunately at my doorstep he was hailed from afar by Paul leaving a taverna and holding up his Frisbee that glinted in the sun. Hy apologized and skittered off. I could see who he preferred! What luck!

"You look like a Balthus," I exclaimed to Daphne wearing a sheer white gauzy sarong wrapped around her slight body. I could just make out the darker thatch between her fawn-like legs.

"What's a Balthus?" she asked me.

"He's a famous French artist who specialized in painting young beautiful girls." Balthus claimed his interest in them had nothing to do with sex, but rather they were physical incarnations of his spiritual muse. I knew better.

The canvases I painted in Mykonos were unstretched and worked on the way I'd read Bonnard preferred, tacked to a wall. I kept the finished masterpieces under my bed in a big roll which I unfurled as we both sat next to each other on its coverlet. As Daphne admired them one after another, I inched closer and closer to her oiled leg covered with the finest adolescent fuzz. She smelled like Coppertone.

"These are beautiful," she said so innocently that I knew she meant it. "The colors are so mysterious and deep." I felt no need to apprise her of the fact that I had accidentally varnished a batch of them with a shellac normally sold for boat decks and, consequently, they had all turned into golden sunsets á la Claude Lorrain.

"You would honor me some day if I could use you as a model to immortalize this summer," I said in a way to emphasize my humility. It didn't come naturally. "You are so wonderfully thin."

"I wish I weren't. My bones stick out, and I don't need a bra."

"I consider that a plus, not a minus." Her laugh was a tinkle of appreciation. She told me she would consider my request, and skittered off to the beach. I performed the act of Pan that evening in her honor.

The next day Paul unfurled what looked like a bedspread from India on the sand large enough to seat his entire retinue. Hy and some girls lay next to the lyre. When I approached Daphne she covered her mouth as if she didn't want me to eavesdrop while she spoke with another beauty.

"Nick, just in the nick of time. Let's all go swim," Paul said as he stood up, tugged at his privates and dived into the water followed by all his gamboling nymphs and Hy except for Daphne.

"I decided I wouldn't mind being immortalized," she said as she twisted a lock of hair around her finger and smiled with a touch of wolfishness that promised something extra might be on the menu, or so I hoped.

We set up a time that same afternoon but before we could chat further Paul came barreling back out of the sea and shook his long blonde locks like a wet dog. Of course the water was aimed at Daphne who giggled and moved away from the damp part of the blanket and me. Later I saw Paul whisper something in her ear and she reared back. What had he said?

When Daphne arrived I began sketching her in the white gauzy nymph-like raiment she wore all the while building up her ego with comments—actually meant, for a change—about her perfect archetypal proportions.

"What's archetypal mean?" she asked.

"To make a long story short, Plato," (*who's Plato*, she didn't ask), "theorized that every form on earth is a reflection of a perfect example of it in heaven. The closer your arm is to that perfect arm, the more beautiful." I took the opportunity to lift her bare appendage (she did not resist) with one hand and with a finger, trace its shallow curves and muscles. Pretending objectivity, I said, "See, an artist follows these lines with his pencil or brush, idealizing a bit, and that's how beauty arrives. When you have a great arm like yours, it is a lot easier."

Daphne seemed to reflect on my statement, rubbing her arm and putting on a dreamy face.

"One day I will ask to draw you nude and the sum of all your curves will be a true masterpiece."

"I don't know if I could," she answered, tentatively enough to assure me that she would. "I guess since we see each other without clothes on the beach it wouldn't make any difference." *The difference*, I thought, *was that it would be in my room.* A half hour later she was lying naked on my bed, holding up a teddy bear I used frequently to so-to-speak, break the ice.

"What was Paul up to?" I asked as I sketched Daphne's form as she stretched cat-like on her back.

"He said I should be careful about getting too close to you. He also tried to kiss my ear."

"Are you afraid of him? Are you a virgin?" I added in a fit of inspiration. Daphne blushed but did not answer. "There's nothing wrong with being a virgin," I said. "Everyone starts like that, and everyone makes the transition to being a beloved except maybe nuns, or really uglies." Daphne laughed and again looked dreamy.

"Will I be a beloved?" she asked as she stared at her reflection in the mirror I use to check my compositions by reversing them. I continued to sketch until my fingers began to cramp.

"I hope we can do this again," I said as she donned her

wrap and traipsed out into a late afternoon sun that still warmed the sand and calm sea in front of my bungalow. Lengthening shadows brought out the primeval elements of the jumble of volcanic rock, granite boulders, and oleander bushes that grew in dried up gulleys behind the beach. Her farewell kiss to my cheek landed accidentally on my lips and it stung like a bee.

Our platonic relationship progressed from drawings to paintings. As her namesake Daphne pursued by Apollo and metamorphosing into a laurel tree. As Galatea steering dolphins for her father, the Old Man of the Sea.

"Do I really look like that," she said more than once, transfixed like Narcissus, and I always replied that she appeared better than that, but no artist could rival the gods who created her. Each time she left me, she gave me a tighter hug. When I was alone I observed my aging carapace in the mirror and wondered if Daphne could love me in the ways I darkly imagined.

By now my relationship with Paul seemed to be settled by our mutual adoration of the opposite halves of the golden pair. Increasingly he devoted his singing to stanzas of an epic he was creating (*of Homeric proportions*, he said with a grin) about Hy and his imagined adventures with a certain lyred friend. The girls began drifting away to pursue prospects with baser intentions than Paul's fairy dust.

One early morning I could not sleep and just after dawn broke I strolled down the beach and over rocks to a room-sized and secluded cove where I could swim and be alone. Today Paul and Hy were already there, embracing each other's wet bodies. After an initial shock, I ducked behind some oregano smelling bushes and watched their play develop to the point that I couldn't resist joining in from my hiding place and began pleasuring myself too. I sneaked back to my bungalow and slept soundly until noon.

"How is your relationship going with Hy?" I asked Daphne at our next session as off-handedly as I could.

"Lately he seems to be drifting away. I think that poem Paul is writing has turned his head. He doesn't want to meet alone anymore. He tells me he needs more space but he still loves me."

"Do you love him?" I asked.

"I guess. I don't know. Maybe. There are lots of people I love, in a way."

Ah, the ambiguity of youth. Perhaps I should take the bull by the horns.

"Could you ever love someone older than yourself?" Daphne stared into space - for the immature, I'd noticed a way to show they are contemplating deeply.

"I suppose I could love someone who's nineteen or twenty."

"What about someone even older who could give you experience?"

"Like you?" Daphne asked. I blushed. She touched my cheek and said, "You are so sweet." Nobody calls a potential lover "sweet." I was crushed. I decided to take another tack that worked for me in the past.

A day or two later I approached a girl with another classical name, Artemis. Some said she was a lesbian because she hung out with a bevy of them, but I know that shy girls often temporarily follow that route. She was easier to convince to pose than Daphne when I found out she loved dogs and cats. A couple of stray felines had taken to hanging out at my doorstep for handouts and with the excuse of her seeing them, I lured her in and showed her some of my work with Daphne.

"I could do that!" she said, showing a competitive side. "Not nude, though," she added.

"Let's try a few preliminary sketches," I said, knowing full well Daphne was scheduled to show up momentarily. Daphne was rendered speechless when she undid my latch and, without knocking, walked in. She managed an "excuse me" before exiting as precipitously as she could. I yelled after her to wait but my operatic outburst was swallowed by the wind. Of course this made Artemis all the more interested in scheduling further appointments. It proved frustrating because Artemis meant it when she said she could only undress with her female friends. I had to use my imagination when I painted certain details of her sturdy and tomboyish body.

When I found Daphne later, she appeared peeved. "Don't say a word to anyone, especially Artemis but there is no contest – you are the most beautiful," I said, to bring her back into my fold. I was becoming an ersatz Casanova – all this emotional activity and sweet talk coming to nothing in the flesh. I began to grow a beard.

The summer progressed from sunny July full of promise to the heavier light of August. The last peak of the summer was the Panagyra, a festival on August fifteenth, ostensibly for the Virgin Stella Maris, but in older times honoring all the gods. It was celebrated in the town square of Ano Mera, the one rural town on Mykonos, and involved a lot of drinking and caterwauling. Unfortunately this year things would get out of hand.

Paul's coterie had shrunk pretty much to Hy – they went into the water in tandem, lay huddled on the beach together, and in general showed indifference to anyone else by staring at each other and intertwining their fingers for hours at a time. I thought this behavior rather teenage-like on Paul's part and wondered what Hy saw in the seductive gravy Paul spewed to the accompaniment of his lyre and his ever-present Frisbee.

Although I wasn't there, this is what I heard happened. Paul and Hy both drank too much ouzo at the evening party, danced the ancient crane dance with the locals (a line of men dipping and sidestepping as you may have seen in the movie about Zorba), then, high as kites, decided to take advantage of a full moon to go down to the beach for a cooling dip. Afterwards, they threw the golden Frisbee back and forth as their naked bodies cast long shadows in the moonlight. And the longest shadow out of Hades took Hy home when attempting to reach the disk as it veered off to the sea, he slipped and bashed his head on underwater rocks lurking close to the shore. A friend going for a dawn swim stumbled across Paul weeping over Hy's beautiful dead body. Appropriately Paul had found some hyacinths growing among the oleanders behind the beach and formed a pillow of them to cradle their namesake's broken skull.

Of course there was a police inquiry but no foul play was determined – a simple accident of the crazy, unanticipated kind that typically happened with foreigners around festival time. Last year a drunken woman with a bottle had attempted to ride down to the beach on the hood of a jeep, fell off, and was run over when the driver backed up to find her without looking into his rear-view mirror. What made me angry was not so much the accident but Paul's lack of remorse. He moaned around muttering clichés in answer to condolences. Something in his voice said he didn't mean it.

"He is in a better place," he told me.

"How could it be better than this. He was beautiful and young. He had a life to live," I said.

"We all have lives," he said. "He will live on in my epic poem, now an elegy to the inevitable loss of love. We all suffer." His attitude reminded me of the old myths in which gods rape and pillage and feast the next day.

Now that Hy was gone Paul's new target was too close to home. Daphne. Just as I was readying the next stage of my assault on her virginal portcullis, he began to interfere. I didn't mind his attempts at flirtation, but did take umbrage at his trash talk about me. "How can you spend time in the wan light of that painter of moonshine when you can be touched by sunbeams," or, more personally, "don't you get tired of Grandpa?" Daphne informed me of everything he said, but I felt she was learning to play me off against Paul.

One afternoon I decided my stand-offishness had gone far enough. After Daphne undressed, gathered the teddy bear and flopped on my bed, I reached out and rearranged one of her downy legs as yet untouched by depilatory or razor. There was no resistance, so I ran my hand up past her dimpled knee. I pretended to slip and touched her bush and then sent my fingers underneath. As if in a trance, she did not move my hand away so I delved deeper. She seemed to stare at my erection plainly visible through the speedo I was wearing, but then she colored and said, "No, no," pushed me away, and sat up protecting her privates with my bear. Her cross look at me made my ardor shrink. "How could you? I thought we were friends."

Despite my protestations and despite her subsequent modeling, it was never the same after that. Daphne's wariness put an invisible barrier between us so high that it began to make me uncomfortable around her. When there is no hope for a conquest, there is a waning of interest. I never believed Dante was being absolutely honest about his feelings for Beatrice.

My prurient daydreams began to switch to Artemis even if I had to imagine what lay beneath her underwear. Like Hy, her sexuality was ambiguous. It became a challenge to try to engage her attention. At first she proved receptive. She was less shy than Daphne and more willing to flirt. Acting the coquette, she would go topless as long as my bungalow's door was open, but gradually her interest in her girlfriends took over and she became "too busy" to pose.

Sadly Daphne drifted away when Paul began a cycle of songs he was to entitle *Paeans to a Virgin.* The first stanzas were recognizably about Daphne, but in each he became more and more enamored of her, claiming his adoration was spiritual, not physical. She represented dawn, the dew of mankind (really!), then became a sunbeam, etc., etc., until a hymn-like dirge which he claimed was not a prophecy but an allegory of Apollo's unrequited love for the nymph Daphne, daughter of the river god Peneius, ended it. One day I accused Paul of plagiarizing Ovid. He smiled at me. "I pity you. Your surname says it all." Daphne was present when he spoke and I could tell she was not at ease with either of us. It turned out she should have been afraid of Paul. Again I learned this at secondhand but apparently they were picnicking next to the Venetian ruins in Ano Mera. Wasps were buzzing around as they finished a bottle of wine and some feta cheese. Paul, made amorous by the way Daphne spit out the black seeds from a wedge of flesh-colored watermelon, leaned over and instead of his lyre's strings, plucked a strap of Daphne's loose shift, which became undone and revealed toasty skin surrounding a fine breast crowned like a cherry dessert by a coral aureole and nipple. He compared it to the chapel atop the hill above them. Daphne's spreading blush made Paul all the more excited. To make up for the confusion he realized he had caused, he placed an oleander flower he had just picked behind her ear.

Daphne brushed it away. "Oleander is poisonous to humans," she said, not getting Paul's implied apology.

"Are you indeed human?" Paul said. "You are like that flower for me. You have poisoned me with love. Kiss me." She pushed him away as he tried to unfasten her other strap.

"Stop it. I'm not ready for that," Daphne said as she arose.

"It has to happen someday. Kiss me," he said again, encircling her torso with his arms. Daphne flinched out of his grasp and ran up the stony path that led to the rounded hill's summit. Paul followed close behind, laughing. As Daphne glanced back in fear, she tripped over the root of a tamarisk tree and fell into a spiky cactus that shredded her perfect skin and brought tears of blood. When Paul reached her, she was unconscious. *Like the Sleeping Beauty*, he thought. When he felt her pulse, there was none.

The usual police procedures cleared the toxic minstrel once again, although they were suspicious of how he could be associated with two mortalities in such a short time. Because of my fear of being tainted by my proximity to him I stayed away for the next several weeks and established myself on other beaches. It was not until a cool breezy day in the middle of September that I saw Paul again – at the center of a circle of girls that included Artemis. When she greeted me it would have looked foolish not to go over. Everyone in the last few days was talking of their plans to leave – Mykonos was a paradise with a due date. No one except the committed or optionless stayed through its notorious off-season rain and gusts.

"Where are you going for the winter, Eclipse?" Paul shouted out. "I'm heading for Hyperborea" he said with a smirk knowing that I would get the reference even if his group did not.

"I thought Hades would be more like it," I said. He ignored my insult.

"I'm taking my new little sister, Artemis. I'm writing some songs for her. We might do a show for Oktoberfest in Munich. All the rest of you girls can act as back-up," he said sweeping his arm around as if bestowing a papal blessing.

That evening by chance I again ran across Paul, this time after dark in the local taverna. When I came out of the WC he motioned me over.

"I know you don't like me but I don't know why. We aren't so different, Eclipse."

"And why is that?"

"You approach life from the dark side. You want mystery. Chiaroscuro. That's why your art is so dark. I want sweet sunshine."

"In the process people get killed. Who's next, Artemis?" I asked.

"Artists like us use up people because our true love is art. If they die around me, is that worse than your wringing them out like suds from a towel and pegging them on a line to dry." I didn't get his analogy but we were interrupted when Artemis came out of the lady's room and put her arm around Paul's waist. "I told Paul about those beautiful sketches you drew of me and he would really like to see them," Artemis said. Was she part of some rapprochement Paul had in mind. *Fat chance*, I said to myself. "Someday" I said to them and lumbered off to my table of one. I tried to chat up the waitress. When that didn't work I ordered another carafe of retsina wine.

Some days later I returned the manuscript to Angelos. "It sounds like fiction to me. Mykonos is not so big that I wouldn't have heard gossip about the mishaps. As Eclipse notes it is also so obviously parallel to tales from Ovid -Apollo accidentally killing his lover Hyacinthus and chasing Daphne. God knows what his next chapter would have been. Remember how the hunter Actaeon accidentally came upon Artemis and her nymphs bathing naked in the woods. She turns him into a stag and sics his own dogs on him."

"I'd like to read that one too," Angelos said, and treated us to another round.

ANDROMEDA

"Let me tell you a tale for midnight," Angelos said. I think his real point was to keep me at the bar until he could order another drink.

A beautiful girl and her mother were neighbors of a friend of mine who lives in Ano Mera. He had no idea what was happening in their household although there was a lot of noise, slamming doors, and once a pillow came sailing out a window. The daughter left the island soon after these events transpired and I only know the story because one of my old girlfriends visited her in America.

The girl's mother named her Andromeda but everyone called her Medi. The mother was named Cassiopeia -- If you remember, Cassiopeia was also Andromeda's mother in the classical myth. Cassopeia's father and Medi's grandfather was a classicist who, brilliant like his idol Nietzsche, went mad like the German philosopher, too. Nietzsche's mistake was that he valued the god Dionysus above all else. Cassopeia's father substituted Apollo for Dionysus in that role but it had the same effect. Too much rationality proved as debilitating to his health as too much wildness.

Some said that Cassopeia had taken on traits both from the myth and her father. Somehow she made a false connection between her daughter's blooming beauty and her own, fading beneath a spider web of wrinkles. When creams and unguents didn't work she tried punishment as if her daughter had stolen what was rightfully hers. Then it got out-of-hand.

Andromeda's upbringing was unleavened by the presence of her father for he had died by his own hand shortly after her twelfth birthday. Later she was told he had been a brilliant scholar also with mental problems who had self-exiled himself to Mykonos and its then obscure village of Ano Mera where he could stretch his drachmas and find the least legal resistance to his irregularities. She was raised off-handedly by her mother who tried to instill in Medi her own belief in a fortune teller whom Cassopeia paid to turn the cards for her frequently. Like her father and grandfather she also began to develop mental irregularities. She claimed her wisdom came from Apollo and that she followed the path of Artemis. Simple people on the island were convinced the family was cursed, others more sophisticated ascribed it to genetics.

I myself can vouch that the fortuneteller herself was thought crazy because she lived alone in squalor with her cats and chickens and considered a goat her familiar. Most who consulted her did not take her scrying all that literally, nor did they return. Cassopeia did.

That is why one afternoon at Agrari, a tourist from Brooklyn named Isaac following his errant Frisbee back behind the beach, through boulders that littered a dry gulley filled with reeds, oleanders, and snakes, found a girl of about his age chained to a rock. Apparently – it was learned later from the fortuneteller herself– Cassopeia had been told that exposing Medi to the god Helios from dawn to dusk would transfer some of her beauty to her mother.

Medi went along with the ordeal to assuage her mother but knew full well her methods were off the beaten track, to say the least.

"Who did this? Should I call the police?" asked Isaac urgently. He stared at the beautiful Medi, dressed only in a dirty white chemise.

"It is an idea of my mother. Don't tell anyone. My mother left the key underneath that bush," she said, pointing.

Isaac unlocked Medi from her shackles and complimented her on her English. She proceeded to explain as best she could why her mother had chained her Prometheus-like to a rock.

"Do you ever go swimming on the beach?" he asked.

"Mother says that is for foreigners."

"How about, since I rescued you, you consider me a friend?" Isaac growing up in a borough of ethnic neighborhoods had experience with odd beliefs. One neighbor kept chickens he ritually strangled on Santeria holidays, another, an Orthodox Jew who couldn't venture out on holy days nevertheless paid Isaac to bring him heroes from the local Italian deli containing pork sausages. Ignoring their eccentricities seemed to work best.

Medi smiled in a diffident twenty year-old way. She boldly told Isaac she worked nights at a taverna but she could meet him next to the road before it descended to the beach at noon the following day. Isaac was cute and seemed polite – not at all like the macho village men who desired her for breeding purposes.

"You must keep it quiet. I'm not supposed to go out with foreigners."

"Don't worry," Isaac said as he re-chained Medi to her Promethean roost. "I'm sure no one will see."

She wore clothes over her bathing suit when she hopped on the back of his scooter, far enough from town that she wouldn't be observed. Her long black hair curled in the breeze as they descended to the glittering waves of a choppy sea. The air was so clear you could see the islands of Naxos and Paros twenty miles across the dark Aegean.

What Isaac failed to ask was if Medi was O.K. with bathing on a beach that tolerated nudity.

"I've heard about it but never seen it," said Medi, when he brought it up. "I'm allowed to come down here only in winter."

Isaac suppressed a giggle when Medi unveiled her swimwear. It was a one-piece decorated with ruffles – too many of them, as if she was in a time warp from the 1950's. Isaac kept on his bathing trunks at first.

After they found a place for their towels, they ran into the clear water and splashed about near the shore because Medi couldn't swim. When they returned they lay on their towels in their wet outfits.

"Why don't we remove them like everyone else?" Isaac said.

It took all of Isaac's power of persuasion and a good hour before she finally relented. Unlike Isaac's overall toast color, Medi possessed an ivory body with a brown face and forearms. Isaac couldn't take his eyes off her. At first she replicated the pose of those statues of Aphrodite slightly stooped, protecting her privates and bust with adroitly placed arms. After another interlude in the sea she strode out of the foam like the birth of the goddess herself.

"I never knew how good it feels," she said as she lay on her back, arms pillowing her head and with most of her skin exposed for the first time in her life to Apollo's rays.

"Let me spread some suntan lotion on you before you burn," Isaac said, throwing out a line he'd used to good effect for years.

Her breasts were firm and small, her body was taut like an athlete's and she had washboard ribs. It was all he could do to keep himself down. Medi noticed it though. His rubs became borderline caresses. Their attraction to each other grew through the afternoon as if it had a life of its own. It was an experience Isaac had never had before, to say nothing of Medi.

When they parted later at the top of the hill Medi kissed him more passionately than he expected and they arranged to meet the next day. He would take the caique to the beach and she would walk down from her home to Agrari beach. It was her night off and this way they could ride the caique together back to town and have dinner. Her jealous mother was told Medi was helping out at a wedding banquet in town.

Again they basked on the beach. A light breeze from the north blew over their wet bodies and caused them both to shiver in delight. Isaac noticed it hardened Medi's nipples. He also saw some ribbons of red welts on her back that were not there yesterday. She did not volunteer where they came from.

She had brought a white dress of loosely woven cotton, typical garb for women on Mykonos then, which she put on behind a bush as they prepared to leave. In those days, if you remember, all the shops ever stocked were white dresses, hand-knitted woolen sweaters and black fishermen's hats that looked like what Russian commissars wore.

"What's wrong?" Isaac asked when she came out. "You look beautiful."She hesitated. "The boatman."

The boatman blew on a conch shell to indicate he had arrived as he drove his prow onto the sand. His burly, hairy body was crammed into a Speedo, and after dropping an anchor off the stern he dove into the water.

"I know him. He is Costa, the boyfriend of my mother. He's going to tell he saw me here."

"Don't worry. I'll take care of you," Isaac said with more bravado than he felt. After his exhibition the boatman blew his conch shell again and announced, "Las Bot." It was nearing six o'clock and the shadow of a hill between the descending sun and the shore was lengthening. Most of the tourists folded their towels, gathered their paraphernalia and clambered onto its deck.

Isaac and Medi had no other choice but to board, too. They ran the gauntlet of a scowling Costa who did not acknowledge he knew Medi. He took the drachma notes from Isaac without uttering a word. Isaac following Medi groped his way onto a free spot atop a small cabin. Costa using his foot steered the caique along the coast, stopping at two other beaches, Super Paradise and Paradise to pick up more passengers before depositing everyone at Platy Gialos where the bus to town waited.

Medi seemed apprehensive the entire way, not speaking but staring into the dark water. When they arrived Isaac was the last to debark. Before he could step onto the dock and catch up with Medi, Costa came up behind him.

"It is no good for you to go out with that girl, my friend. Be smart." He hissed like a snake.

Isaac did not respond, instead stepped up his pace and caught up with Medi still half pretending they weren't together.

"I'm afraid of him. He has a bad temper," Medi said. On the bus the few miles into town she seemed quiet. "I just want to be like the tourists," she said as they sat at a café on the port. "They're not forced to wear black. They don't have mothers."

Isaac took Medi to Joanna's a taverna he knew on the outskirts of the port. It was on a usually windy beach because it faced north but this evening the sea had turned to glass. They entered it from a doorway flush on a busy street and found an empty table set up on the sand a few meters from the water.

Isaac let Medi do the ordering in Greek but it made no difference. The same dishes he would have ordered arrived all at once. A *horiataki, melatzani salata, keftedes* and at Isaac's insistence a carafe of *retsina*. Medi told him only tourists ordered the pine-flavored wine.

They sat and watched the sun go down on another day in the history of the world. By the time the carafe was empty, stars shone in a night sky. Isaac took Medi's hand and held it under the table. Their conversation consisted of rehearsed histories, not long because most of their lives had not yet unspooled, but filled with the hope young romances bring. Yes, Isaac felt he was falling in love and judging from her eyes so did Medi.

"Everything you say about what you want out of life is what I want too," Medi said fondling his wrist.

"I can't believe we are so alike, coming from such different places and all. I feel like I can finish your sentences," Isaac said.

"Somewhere up there is the constellation called Andromeda," Medi said, "but I've never been able to locate it." Isaac could not help her.

After Isaac paid the bill they strolled the beach and, as in movies they'd seen, embraced and kissed again and again. Medi told her mother the wedding would last into the night so she would sleep over in town in the house of a relative. Since this was before the age of cell phones – in fact since there was no phone service where she lived at all, no one could check up on her. Remember those days when the sole available telephones on the island were in the OTC office – you had to pay in advance while an operator dialed. Only when your party was reached were you ordered into one of several booths.

It was not hard to convince Medi to spend the night in Isaac's room, whose window framed the row of famous windmills, the symbol of Mykonos that appears on travel posters. His room had a separate entrance at the top of a staircase on the outside of his landlady's house. They were observed going up.

That hot, nearly airless night they lay in bed unclothed, covered only by a sheet. They cuddled and kissed but Medi was not ready for the ultimate step. She was still a virgin, she said, and Isaac did not want to push her. Love can make delayed gratification even sweeter. Isaac rubbed his hands over the ridges of her backbone. He squeezed her buttocks and ran his finger between their intertwined bodies past her stomach into her pubic hair but stopped short at the cleft.

"I've never felt one before," Medi said as Isaac pressed himself against her and encouraged her to take his erect penis in her hand. He was dying to tell her to move her hand up and down but she held it tightly as if it were a motorcycle handle. There was little sleep. All night, they lay in wonderment at what had happened so quickly.

Since Medi worked evenings the newly amorous couple had most of the next day together before she had to be back in Ano Mera. Isaac decided to drive out on rutted roads to a beach on the unfrequented north side of Mykonos. Called Mersinna it possessed one small vacation house improbably owned by a Methodist minister from Atlanta. It was usually deserted. Next to it on another beach called Fokos was a quiet taverna Isaac planned for lunch.

Isaac's scooter raised a cloud of dust as they bounced along by the island's reservoir. Isaac accelerated as fast as his machine would go – he didn't want to be left in anyone's dust and in his rear view mirror he saw a cloud of it unfurling some way back.

They were happily alone when they scanned the beach from a hill above it where Isaac parked the scooter. They jogged down to the shore stripping off clothing as they moved, plunged directly into the cool briny water of their private cove and, paying attention to nothing else, splashed and kissed and played with each other's bodies.

When they finally staggered over pebbles and out of the water their towels and possessions were not where they had left them. Isaac looked up at the top of the hill and fortunately found that his scooter was still there. As they stood naked and shivering a man appeared from behind the minister's house.

He lumbered as if he were drunk as he approached. Medi put her hand over her mouth.

"It is Costa," she said.

Costa screamed something in Greek to Medi. He called Isaac, a "*malacca*," which Isaac knew was as bad as it gets oath-wise.

He rushed Isaac before he could register what was happening. Costa aimed a roundhouse punch but missed and clipped his shoulder. It was painful enough that Isaac saw red and punched Costa back in the stomach but to little effect. It was obvious the boatman was larger and stronger. Their struggle became a match between a staggering Goliath and a feinting David until with one blow of a rock to the head held by Medi, Costa went down. They were afraid to approach him at first. His body twitched for a time, then it stopped and the one eye not covered by blood oozing from his wound stared at the sand.

The two lovers' adrenaline was flowing as they went over to Costa's prone body.

"I guess we got him," Isaac said with a quavering voice.

Medi felt for a pulse. "He's dead."

Words were so inadequate to how they felt in the proximity of death that they said nothing more. The wind in Mykonos usually blows from the north out of the Balkans when it is called the *meltemi.* That day it was a strong south wind – from the Sahara and Africa. The two lovers pulled the boatman's bulk to the water and his corpse soon bobbed out to sea beyond half-submerged rocks that myth said caused the shipwreck of Ajax returning from Troy. They sat on the beach silently panting from their exertions and watched Costa disappear.

As if stung by the same bee, they grabbed each other in a passion neither had known before. They kissed desperately. Isaac plunged into her salt-stained body for the first time and they tore at each other like fighting lions. When they finished they found their clothes hidden behind the house along with Costa's motorcycle which they left alone.

"Let's pretend nothing happened," Medi said. "Let's not go to the taverna at Fokos. That way no one will know we were ever nearby."

Isaac appreciated her cold bloodedness. In books it was usually the man less affected by murder and mayhem but Isaac felt so queasy he feared he would throw up. They scootered back to Ano Mera, passing no one. Isaac let Medi off before he reached the main road that led to the port, and she walked home also unobserved. They agreed not to meet for several days.

Costa obviously did not return. Cassopeia muttered that he'd probably met a foreign girl and was holed up in the port. After another day she heard from a boatman who lived nearby that Costa's caique had taken on water at its mooring due to the unusual south wind. It was unlike him to neglect his boat.

The police were notified the evening of the second day and Cassopeia became increasingly anxious. Medi observed silently.

On the third day Costa's motorcycle was found by the minister who had just returned from leading a group of pilgrims to the cave of St. John on Patmos. He called the tourist police thinking it might have been a deserted rental.

When Cassopeia was told Costa's motorcycle was found but

he was still missing, she feared the worse. She knew he would never leave his boat and his motorcycle unattended. The police became convinced Costa had taken a swim and drowned. A heart attack? Perhaps. He was known to be a heavy drinker. Nobody knew anyone who had been on Mersinna that day.

"My love. My love," Caasopeia keened over and over. "Why aren't you sad?" she asked Medi.

"He was not nice to me."

"How could you not like him," Cassopeia said. "He was your father."

Medi was floored "Why did you never tell me?"

"Costa had a wife when you were born." And after all you are my daughter and I wanted to protect you.

Her mother in the company of other village women wept, wailed and gossiped into the night. Medi meanwhile waited until her waitressing hours were over and hitch hiked into town. She found Isaac in his room.

The look on her face drew his embrace. "It's over, Medi. We're both O.K."

"It is more complicated than that," Medi said, and told him what she had heard.

Isaac did not answer right away. *What was it called, patricide when a son kills his father? Was it the same word for a daughter?* Isaac noticed her emotions were so conflicted she could not describe them to him, except by making love again and again.

"I am free of my mother, too," Medi said.

They spent the rest of the night plotting their future. They left Mykonos that week never to return except in the chains of their memories.

CIRCE

For a change Angelos and I agreed to meet at the bar at Remezzo, a chic disco with a spectacular view of the harbor. The action along with the sound volume turned higher later in the evening but we were here to ogle the beauties who come forth like mosquitos at dusk to sting Greek ship owners and Russian gangsters and hope for a dinner invitation.

"I know that fellow down the bar," Angelos said. "He lives on a modest trust fund sufficient to allow him to pretend he is a working poet."

"Is that Jim Forester?" Angelos said loudly, his voice booming over the soft rock.

"I'm doing what you're doing," Jim said with a slur the result of several scotches.

"Tell my friend that crazy story about Circe, the improbably named girl you met here once," Angelos asked him, after a bout of small talk. "You'll love to hear this." "She was more beautiful than anyone I've seen tonight" Jim said. "And lethal," Angelos added. "Enough" I said. "I have to hear it."

O.K. Some time ago I was checking out the scene at Remezzo when my eyes locked on one woman who arrived with an entourage of bullet-headed men sporting earplugs. My companion at the bar was Carlos Panos, who knew everybody and everything. Carlos's father had signed over a few tankers to him from his fleet when he turned twenty-one and then ignored his son while he pursued expensive Scandinavian mistresses and even more expensive impressionist art. Carlos in turn had ignored the tankers. This made his fortune since he had leased them long-term at just the right moment to a major international oil company.

"Would you like to meet her?" Carlos asked me when he noticed my focus.

"Why not?" I replied, and quaffed a mouthful of beer.

"You must be careful with this one. She was the mistress of an arms merchant from one of the former SSRs – Belarus I think. He was shot in mysterious circumstances in Rwanda and she managed to secure his fortune. She comes from somewhere up north near Salonika but no one knows much about her. Even her name must be made up - she calls herself Circe. She is said to eat men—they always disappear after a brief fling. They never last."

"Quite a challenge," I said as Carlos walked over to her group at a prime table next to the dance floor. Carlos loved to show his power to actuate circumstances. I suppose being Greek allowed him to pretend to be the universal host.

"She will dance with you," Carlos said when he returned.

When I took her arm under the intense scrutiny of her companions, I was intoxicated by her smell – a perfect blend of perfume and a musky aroma that emanated from her body.

"Why haven't we met before?" I said staring into her eyes in the way that'd always worked for me.

"I haven't been here for awhile," she replied, in an odd accented English as if her teacher was a Bulgarian who'd learned it from a Frenchman. "I have an island off the coast near Corfu. Aeaea. I stay there most of the time." She was indeed a high roller.

"Well then, why bother coming to Mykonos at all?" I asked, tightening my arm against the stretch of skin revealed by her backless dress.

"To meet people like you," she said, and laughed.

We danced through several sets, ending with a slow romantic Sinatra number. By this time, I was stroking her velvety back as surreptitiously as I could in the shadowy club.

Circe did not invite me back to her table, but she did ask me to visit her at home "by the pool" the following afternoon. "I'll leave word at the gate to let you in."

"She's a handful," I said to Carlos when he rejoined me at the bar. "So, she owns an island called Aiaia?"

"I've never heard of it," Angelo interjected "but it was quite chic to own an island at one time. It put you in the same league with Onassis and Niarchos. Now high rollers would rather show off in a big yacht."

I never could pass up an invitation. I figured the "danger"

associated with her was the result of men being fearful of rejection in going after such a beauty. Besides I like adventure. The next afternoon I found myself bouncing in my jeep driving the few miles out of town to an area called San Stefano. Just north of its beach, beyond a cluster of tavernas was a large dark structure I had thought was a high-end hotel. The complex unlike most of Mykonos had dark stone walls and bronze tinted windows but it was spectacular, perched on a shelf overlooking the Aegean. I'd seen a helicopter land there once which I imagined was ferrying clients from Athens.

As I now discovered, it was all Circe's. A female "secretary" met me at the front gate and led me through the compound to a huge swimming pool. Circe lounged in a yellow bikini that set off her bronzed skin under a canopy that appeared to be made of sewn-together Hermes scarves. "I commissioned it," she said. All these colors together remind me of Matisse."

The "secretary" directed me to a changing room, where I donned a bathing suit and was given a towel, before returning to my hostess and the chair she patted beside her. "I don't bite," Circe said when she noticed my defensive posture as I sat down.

After a mojito and a swim together in the pool I was more relaxed. In fact I couldn't take my eyes off her. I was especially excited by her unshaven underarms. I found the little tufts of black hair incredibly sexy. I surmised she was a superbly well-taken-care-of thirty. Her body looked younger and her face was unlined (Botox?) but a certain hardness of experience showed in her features.

Towards sundown she excused herself, saying she had to attend to some business, but asked me to meet her at Kalo Livadi Beach the next day for lunch at Sol y Mar, one of the "in" tavernas that year. On weekends it was a meat market, as bikinied beauties from Athens paraded through, showing off their oiled curves in search of husbands and sugar daddys.

Usually one would say at this point that we spent the day on the beach getting to know each other but in this case it was not strictly accurate. Her conversation was limited to the here and now. "What is that drink?" "The woman shouldn't wear purple," that sort of thing. When I asked about her past, I was deflected by "Oh, it was too long ago" or "where I grew up was so boring I can't even remember it." At the same time she was endlessly seductive, "accidentally" brushing against me (once, underwater, against my crotch), pretending indifference behind her sunglasses but watching me watch her.

"Why don't you come by for another drink this evening? We can dine together, just the two of us. I'll show you my hobby, a little menagerie of animals. We travel together wherever I go."

On my return to the port in the late afternoon, I found Carlos hovering over an early drink at one of the harbor side cafes. I updated him on my experiences with Circe. "I bet she is going in for the kill. Here's a bit of advice, my friend. You'll think you won't need it but take a Cialis pill before you go" Carlos reached into his wallet and popped one out from an aluminum container. "You'll thank me."

When I arrived at her compound that evening I noticed Circe had set up a table but instead of chairs, had placed couches with pillows around like pictures I'd seen of how classical Greeks partied. I wondered how comfortable that would be with the tight white jeans I wore, until I noticed crinkly pajama pants folded on one of the sofas. She had thought of everything. Needless to say, after a dinner composed of a cornucopia of seafood – lobster, sea urchins, scallops and Dover sole washed down with Chassagne-Montrachet and prosecco—Circe and I were halfway there. For dessert, she moved over to my couch and popped strawberries into my mouth. I imagined this is what it must have felt like to be an innocent virgin seduced by Casanova. She was relentless.

102

"What about the menagerie you wanted to show me? I've never seen a zoo on Mykonos, except at two in the morning," I feebly joked.

"That can wait," she said, and thrust her tongue into my mouth. She was savage when she made love. She writhed. She scratched. She screamed. She rolled her eyes until all I saw was white when she had an orgasm. We lay on the couch panting in a pool of sweat. Then she asked for more.

Thank God for the inventor of Cialis, I thought, as I managed to respond. After the second session we dipped into the pool and floated watching slow blinking lights of airplanes high overhead, making their way from Athens to Cairo or Dubai across the starry sky. Her servants were so discreet that had I'd forgotten they existed, until dry towels appeared mysteriously when we exited the pool. Had they been watching? Perhaps that turned her on, too.

When we were dry, Circe beckoned for me to follow her into a space so vast that the bed it contained seemed lost. She asked me to rub an aromatic oil into her skin. She offered to do the same for me.

"It contains an aphrodisiac," she said.

I dozed off after that but awoke in the middle of the night to her ministrations again. The muscles that manipulated my own tongue felt sore as I repaid the compliment. Again we made love and again fell asleep.

Just before dawn broke I opened my eyes when I heard a cock crow.

"Is that part of your menagerie?" I asked Circe who was wide awake beside me, tickling my balls with her fingers.

"Come, I'll show you."

Naked we padded across a courtyard in the still night air to another building. It was filled with the sounds of snoring and stirring when we entered. I expected to see the animals one would associate with a private zoo – a chimpanzee, perhaps a young lion

103

cub, but here was a herd of bristly black pigs, a woodpecker she called Picus and several goats – nothing I would really call wild.

"These are my old boyfriends," Circe said matter-of-factly. She didn't laugh but I did. At the same time I vaguely recalled how Circe in the *Odyssey* had turned some of Odysseus' men into swine.

Circe stared at me in a strange way. Her face changed into an unearthly grimace, and I knew my dalliance with her was ended—even Cialis wouldn't help me recover from that.

"Watch me. I will show you the most erotic dance you've ever seen."

Using a sarong as a prop and two castanets she writhed like a snake and sang an eerie song. She sang it slow like a sea chantey with the speed lowered.

As she held her arms over her head like Carmen clicking castanets, I focused on her underarms, which I had drenched with kisses hours before. I felt the twitch of seduction but I knew something was not right.

As she danced on, I did something shocking. To this day, I don't know why. It might have been my instincts taking over, my guardian angel or just fear, but I stood up and pretended to dance in tandem behind her. When she turned to me she smiled triumphantly as if she had won. I grabbed her sarong, wrapped it around her neck and carried her back to her bedroom. She kicked and yelled but fortunately it was too early for any servants to be up. I tied her wrists and ankles to the bed using rope I'd grabbed passing the Hermes canopy. "I like that," Circe said in a voice that caressed the words. I knew what she imagined would follow. Instead I gathered my clothes and vaulted over a stone fence on a shortcut down to San Stefano Beach. Dawn was lighting up the sky as I drove the deserted highway back to the port and the safety of my room. "So how was it, with her?" Panos asked me with a smirk the next day. "All I can say is thank God you gave me that pill."

"I still can't figure her out," Jim said as he ordered another scotch. "Later by chance I saw her feeding a small fish she'd just bought at the market adjacent to his usual perch to Petros the pelican mascot of Mykonos. I said 'hi' but she looked at me behind her sunglasses as if I didn't exist."

Nymphs of Mykonos

"What a surprise to see you. You told me, you weren't coming back?" said my old friend Angelos, whom I'd accidentally encountered by the waterfront as I humped a wheeled suitcase off the ferry from Piraeus on a cloudless June morning. "How many years ago was that?"

"Mykonos is too much a part of me, I can't stay away" I replied. "I begin daydreaming about summer here when the gray months kick in, but this time I'm earlier. What's new?" I asked.

"The peripheral road to the new marina is finally in use and there are speed bumps in front of the school but otherwise it is still the strawberry season." We have a standing axiom that when peaches replace strawberries with our ice cream at cafes along the port the high season has truly begun.

That evening over a drink at Vengera, then hopping as the café of choice for our crowd, Angelos quizzed me on the course of my artistic career.

"If you remember when we first met, I was working on painting the island as it is. Now I've branched off into imagery from myths - Apollo and Daphne, Pan and Syrinx; events that could have happened here. I've tried my hand at writing, too; some things can't be expressed by a brush."

"Why don't you write about the old days, when we were young and desirable," Angelos said with a laugh. "Life was so simple then."

"As a matter of fact, I have. About my first visit, before I'd even met you. I wrote it in the third person to emphasize my youthful naiveté and made myself an Italian. Would you like to read it? I'll give you a copy tomorrow."

Mykonos was the place to be that summer, at least that's what *Vogue* said. Models dressed in white beach wraps posed in several magazine spreads before the deep blue sea and dusty buff colored hills of the Cyclades—Greek islands of which Mykonos was the crown jewel. Giorgio had heard his own siren call in the spring when he left his boring job teaching English to idiots in Padua to finally do what he'd always wanted--paint. He had money enough for a long season saved up, and life as he envisioned it, in a small bungalow on the island's nude and best beach shouldn't cost much.

After several weeks he reflected on his good fortune. His body was tanner, his hair bleached lighter than it had ever been. A daily baptism in the Aegean gave him an ecstatic rush when his wet skin was caressed by the same breeze, called the *meltemi* hereabouts, that kept the water clean, sleep coolly refreshing and the island bug free.

He had just finished his daily quota of two hours work after a late breakfast and began to feel the heat of midday ratchet up to a palpable presence blanketing the thyme and oregano scented hills. The only fly in the ointment were the girls. They came and went as tourists for two or so weeks from all over Europe, but the ones he liked best invariably couldn't stay, and there were dry periods when pretty and available replacements did not arrive. His tastes ran high. It had been two weeks since anything interesting had happened and he was beginning to feel like a swollen mosquito. On the far end of the beach a group of raunchy Parisians, all of indeterminate sexual preference, one of indeterminate sex, had set up an illegal camp. Sylvie was a hermaphrodite, a sylph's body that sported a penis as well as two beautiful breasts and a tattoo of a dragon on her left shoulder.

Most of Mykonos' tourists then did not get up until late morning and since they had to travel to the beach by fishermen's caiques, they did not arrive until after the sun had hit its meridian. So far this morning, except for Giorgio, the Parisians lounging in front of their tent were the only inhabitants. He put his towel down close enough to watch their showy antics but far away enough not to be obvious, and went for a swim in the aqua-colored waters near the shore. When he came out, they passed him on the way to the taverna carrying beach bags made of Indian bedspreads and wearing clothes artfully wrapped and knotted to reveal and cover at the same time. They shouted "Yassou, bonjour" and so did he. Just yesterday Sylvie drunk after lunch had tried to pick him up, her male member swelling slightly as she spoke. Giorgio had been excited by the rich brown breasts artfully framed by a gold neck chain and figa but he was less sure of the goings on down below. In the end it was its Sylvie's coarse quality more than her equipment that kept him from biting.

As Giorgio lay basking on the hot sands, he thought of his art. The truth of it was that this location was not the best for hard work. He was less distracted back home when he sacrificed his social life to evenings painting. But life had to be lived too. There was always autumn back in the Veneto.

He closed his eyes and when he awoke an hour later he was no longer alone. Beach mats and paraphernalia surrounded him as tightly as a hot day on the Lido. Among the bodies that cavorted and sprawled, he spied an almost perfect one he'd never seen before. It was easy to be introduced here, you just went over and said hello, and that's what he did after intercepting a glance that indicated she might be receptive. Her name was Claudia, she came from Munich and she was vague about occupation. Most people look naked with their clothes off but with her even overall tan she was like a Botticelli nude. Her charms were covered only with a towel wrapped around her head (to keep her glossy black hair from drying out, she told him later) and a Cartier watch encrusted with diamonds. The watch had stopped at 11:30 some bygone midmorning or night. She explained she couldn't trust a local jeweler with its repair but Giorgio suspected it had not worked for longer than her arrival here, since she never, even accidentally, consulted it.

The pace of Mykonos was such that by evening they were passionately embracing on its white streets, and by the following morning her perfumed and his suntan lotion smelling skin had thoroughly mingled and impregnated his sheets. She never said much, because English was the only language they had in common, and hers was limited to simple statements. Giorgio had such a fertile imagination that it made her all the more mysterious and desirable.

Claudia drifted away bikini by bikini from her rented room in town until she finally had moved in solidly with Giorgio. She was lazy, she loved to eat and drink, and after every lunch at the taverna with its bottle of retsina, Greek salad and fried calamari, they attacked each other for dessert before a wine-drugged siesta kicked in back at the shuttered bungalow. Claudia was vague about her departure date and kept putting it off. This made Giorgio imagine she liked him all the more and he became infatuated. He liked it that she always insisted on paying her own way and that made him consider her sensitive to his underfunded life. However he wondered if his obsession with her body trumped everything else. Of course his work suffered but that could wait.

This sensual existence ended abruptly two weeks later when after three days of storm warnings in the form of outrageous flirtations between the two, Claudia moved over to the beach blanket of Ken Howard, novelist and fifth husband of Laine Terry, the legendary movie star. Who didn't know the story of Ken and Laine? For a year they were on top of the charts gossip-wise but Laine left for Number Six and a hacienda in Mexico off-the-beaten-track. It was rumored that Ken received alimony but his story was that 1) he was working on a new television series or 2) completing a new sure to be best-selling novel. Whenever he was crossed, which was often (he was a bad drunk), he would say darkly, "Wait till I put you in my new book". His rawboned American charisma made Claudia feel there was a seamless web between her body and Laine Terry's, and from there to a good chunk of Hollywood.

Claudia's clothes moved out of Giorgio's bungalow faster than they had moved in. The last he heard from her was when she stopped to say good-bye on her way to Sardinia and retrieve a bikini bottom he'd found under his bed. Giorgio berated himself more for his lack of understanding of women than sorrow over Claudia's departure. When his feeling of dejection began to wane after the first few days he knew it was just a summer romance and he consoled himself with a too-young but impressionable Bavarian with whom verbal communication was next to nothing. For the moment he felt it was better that way.

Sometime later Giorgio went into town on a morning that was as crisp as fresh laundry. The meltemi was blowing hard, the windmills were creaking, the sapphire blue Aegean had kicked up white caps and the news was that Laine Terry herself had arrived on the island. She had been seen feeding the resident pelican for photographers. She had been observed stepping out of a taxi in front of the Leto Hotel. It was said she looked better than her pictures.

Giorgio had no mail at the *Poste Restante* but he picked up some fruit and newspapers and went back to his bungalow. Instead of the beach he headed to the taverna for an early lunch. The sole diner was an attractive woman in a scarlet beach robe and matching turban. Yes, it was the legendary Laine Terry eating a bowl of yoghurt all by herself. Giorgio couldn't believe his eyes. He nodded when he passed her table and she graciously said hello to him. "I enjoy your movies so much, Miss Terry", he said. He winced at his own banality. She appeared startled. He backed away in embarrassment, blushing. She smiled with the radiance that had been immortalized by the great directors. "I thought you were Greek", she said. He looked about as Greek as Robert Redford. In her help-poor-little-me act that always worked with men, she managed to ask him where the best part of the beach was, and where to eat at night before her chauffeur-bodyguard returned from arranging the rental of a caique for the next day.

She liked him, Georgio could tell. She invited him to lie next to her on the beach. She listened with rapt attention as he bragged about his (up-to-now) barely evident career. When they strolled through town arm-in-arm, people pointed and wondered if he too was a star they had not yet heard of. At night at Remezzo, the most fashionable local disco she danced with her eyes locked on him. The next day her seventh husband, a Swiss manufacturer of chocolate arrived but Laine included Giorgio in the social arrangements. They dined out on lobster every night with a group of six or eight and he was always invited.

One night as they were leaving Remezzo in a taxi hired exclusively for their stay, Laine insisted that Giorgio sit in the back seat with her. "My husband will be more than happy up-front", she said. Giorgio gulped but acquiesced, especially since she had his hand in a tight grip. "I love artists" she said. "Anyone can make money, ONLY YOU CAN CREATE." She spoke in capital letters. When her husband came out to the taxi, after paying everyone's bill, Giorgio pulled his hand away feeling guilty but she grabbed it again. "He doesn't mind", she hissed.

Her husband left the island on urgent business for a few days and Giorgio and Laine spent the night together. For Giorgio it was boring in bed--the screen's sex queen was passive and uninspired. He really didn't like older women anyway, but the thought that he was with Laine Terry and would have a tale to tell kept him going.

The next afternoon a gorgeous tanned young woman, aerobically fit, put down her glittery flight bag and sarong not two meters from his and Laine's location, and Laine with her customary charm included the girl in her immediate entourage. Giorgio could not take his eyes off this toast-colored nymph with hazel eyes. She swam like a mermaid, then sat on a rock.

As she combed water out of her blond streaked hair she caught Giorgio watching and smiled. This was invitation enough for him.

"Are you French?" Giorgio asked in English noticing her bag emblazoned with its Air France logo.

"Oui. I am Nicole. And you?" she asked offering a formal handshake.

"I am Italian but I don't speak French. Are you enjoying Mykonos?"

"I love Greece. I have been travelling in the Peloponnese all summer paying my way by harvesting grapes. In the winter I am a student at the university in Paris."

"That must be hard work, out in the sun all day."

"I love the sun. After work we had wonderful times around the fire," Nicole said batting her eyes. Giorgio was not sure if she was flirting or just having fond memories.

"I know who you are," Nicole said to Laine when Giorgio introduced them. "I am a big fan. I have seen all your cinemas since I was a little girl," she added.

Giorgio wondered if Laine would take that as a compliment or an insult. As the women chatted how they both loved Paris, Giorgio stared at a yacht sailing along out to sea and pretended not to listen. He loved the way Nicole spoke English with that little girl accent only French women could pull off, Giorgio knew this was finally it. Everything she said underlined his emotion. She was the one.

As the afternoon passed in a sunny haze Giorgio bubbled and glowed and spread his dazzling charm like a bright Matisse collage over the beach. His audience was both one of the most beautiful and one of the most famous women in the world. His new infatuation did not escape Laine's attention, however.

When he took Nicole with him to the taverna to pick up some fruit juice, she insisted on taking her flight bag. "Everything I own is in there. It is even big enough for my bikini," she said and giggled. Despite the suggestive tone, he did not allow himself to be led flesh- wards immediately. With true love the appeal had first to be to the soul was his maxim. Why spoil it by falling too quickly into the physical. When they returned and sought their respective beach towels, Giorgio mentioned that he would be at the Vengera Bar in town at nine, and he would love to buy her a drink. With a smile as assent, she said nothing. It said everything to him.

At nine Giorgio was dressed in his best linen pants and shirt open to reveal a gold chain that hung from his neck. White teeth shone from a brown face. He was a resort ad. Nicole suddenly and silently appeared next to him, kissed and accepted a drink. She did not say much at first, just looked modestly down in a way that showed her awareness that every male in the vicinity was trying to get her attention. When Laine showed up late as usual, she animated the place and the evening began. Laine was like an orchestra conductor Giorgio thought as everyone in the presence of fame and charisma ratcheted up their performances imagining themselves as actors in *the* place to be seen.

The evening ended for Giorgio after dinner at Philippi's, a garden restaurant in the middle of town, after an hour of non-stop dancing at Remezzo and after a ride in Laine's taxi out to the beach. She had rented a bungalow alongside Giorgio's there as well as her room in town--to watch the sunrise, she said. Her bodyguard stayed in the port, "to guard my jewels and traveler's checks," she said.

Nicole sat between them in the taxi. Giorgio assumed she was coming to stay with him, and with some alarm was rehearsing reasons and excuses that might satisfy Laine. He knew Laine would be jealous when he finally had to say goodnight and leave her alone. But what could he do? She was older and this was true love. Life must go on. He rationalized furiously trying to think of a more spectacular excuse.

When they arrived at the beach Laine proposed a walk on the beach by moonlight. There was no wind, practically a full moon and the water was lapping gently on the shore; Giorgio stripped off his disco-sweated clothes, the two women followed his example, and plunged with him into the sea. As they frolicked in the murk they left phosphorescent trails. Nicole was worried about *degoutant* creatures coming out of the deep.

They swam to the shore and watched the moon rise higher.

It cast such a glow in the night sky that the ordinarily bright stars around it were obliterated. A pair of blinking lights passed over- -a jetliner on the way from Athens to the Middle East, thought George. They said nothing as the three of them lay naked on their backs on the still warm sand.

When they were dry but deliciously salty, they gathered their clothes and ambled back to the bungalows. Laine entered her bungalow first, lit a candle and came back outside. "Good night, sleep well", she said softly and kissed Giorgio on the lips. *Had she read my thoughts?* Could even Laine see Nicole and Giorgio were meant to be? Laine turned and entered into the soft glow of her doorway again. Giorgio put his hand in Nicole's and held it. Light and dry as a feather. She gently squeezed his, withdrew it, and followed. Her long skirt normally buttoned down the front had turned ninety degrees to the side and like a hospital gown exposed a delectable brown thigh. Slung over her shoulder was a scarf that before, in a complicated tied arrangement, had served as her shirt. Now her arm modestly covered bare breasts in a gesture that reminded Giorgio of a pose favored by ancient sculptors of Aphrodite. Nicole kissed him before entering Laine's door, a vision of loveliness silhouetted by candlelight, and softly said, *"Bon soir Giorgio, A Demain."*

RETURN OF ODYSSEUS

It was late – the sundown crowd who come to the Kastro bar in Mykonos for cocktails and Erik Satie had left for dinner, dancing and if lucky sex. I told Angelos that I had dined well the night before at Kounela's Fish restaurant. I had heard about it for years but thought it just one small courtyard in the labyrinth of streets behind the port promenade. I hadn't realized that there were steps across the narrow lane from the courtyard that led to several expansive, airy second-floor rooms.

Angelos, sipping his usual ouzo, had just finished telling me a story about a gay friend of his who, in the mid-seventies, owned one of the few vehicles on the island. The friend named Bo always travelled with a huge fluffy white poodle and one day upon arriving at Elia Beach, about five miles from town, announced he also had a queen in his camper. "Of course," Angelos said, "we thought he was referring to another gay." Actually he had run across the divorced and exiled Saroya, Queen of Iran hitchhiking and had picked her up.

At that point Yurgos, an archaeologist friend of Angelos strolled in and was introduced to me.

"If this man," he said as he slapped Angelos back, "had not renovated his mother's shop I would never have found my greatest discovery – the giant archaic *pithos* or pot decorated with the first representation of the *Iliad* in art. It is inscribed by the potter in panels like a comic strip complete with the Trojan horse. It made my career"

After we bought Yurgos a drink it led him to a story a part of which took place in the very fish restaurant I had mentioned. Who knows if it is true.

"You know my friends, some scientists theorize that time itself is not a straight chronological line but bends and warps. That would account for premonitions, how the ancient myths can repeat themselves with subtle differences, like a spiral returning but not exactly to the same place. And it may explain how it happened that some sailors spent a brief sojourn here recently who claimed they were on the way home from Troy.

They arrived in a strange black ship. Fishermen on the dock that morning had seen nothing like it and they admired its sleek curved lines and intricate rigging. Its bronze fittings all looked homemade. The furled sail was of a rougher weave than canvas and was dyed a rich purple that had faded except at the edges. A vacationing archaeologist friend of mine said he had seen a ship like this — on a fifth century B.C. Athenian pot. Odysseus was the captain of that one. What a marvelous reconstruction of an ancient vessel, down to the finest details he observed. It was even better than the war trireme recently reconstructed out of Piraeus.

The crew of the black ship slept through a good part of the morning, through the noisy commerce taking place at the fish market and fruit and vegetable stalls immediately adjacent. Japanese tourists from a cruise ship were snapping pictures of the island's mascot Petros the Pelican as he gobbled up fish innards. The bars and cafes along the port were dispensing coffee and late breakfasts to tourists and locals alike.

Altogether it was a peaceful blue day until a feathered arrow from the direction of the boat punctured Petros' heart. There was a moment of disbelief before cacophony broke out.

Into this scene appeared a sailor from the boat brandishing a finely carved bow. He said hello in a language no one understood except the archaeologist — it was like running across an Englishman who still spoke like Beowulf. The bearded sailor resembled a pirate of old, a scarf tied on his head, pants stitched together from leather patches, a fleecy vest, earrings and bracelets gleaming in gold, his sandals laced up to his knees. He approached the pelican, pulled out his arrow and nonchalantly slung its carcass over his shoulder.

One of the fish vendors confronted the pirate, screaming at him in Greek. The recipient of the invective looked blank. Finally the archaeologist approached and tried his ancient Greek. "Where do you come from? Which university?"

The sailor appeared mystified and answered that their home was on Ithaca. They intended to eat the bird. The archaeologist turned to the crowd and recounted this exchange. He was met with laughter.

The pirate shrugged his shoulders and marched back on his ship.

Finally the harbor police arrived and clambered on board the vessel where they were met by a band of five of its crew along with its captain. The captain was distinguished from his sailors by a breastplate echoing the curves of his front torso in bronze. He had knotted little ribbons in his beard. Of course the foreign sailors had no idea what the police, joined by the harbor master, were saying.

"There is no request from you to dock here. You have no flag. Who are you?" the harbor master asked. "There are fees to pay, papers to fill out. You cannot just show up. Are you Turks?"

He was met with blank incomprehension and then like a call to arms as they fingered their bows and broadswords until the archaeologist wormed his way between them. "They say they are coming from Ephesus. That was an important ancient city but it is now just an archaeological zone."

The captain sizing up the situation reached into a pouch and pulled out five silver coins. He held his arm out to the harbormaster. The archaeologist picked several off the captain's palm and examined them in disbelief.

"This is an Athenian coin from about 500 BC. See, on one side is a bust of Athena, on the reverse her symbol, the owl. It is worth a lot – mint condition. And this one is Ephesian. Note the bee."

By now everyone thought it was an elaborate joke. Some speculated that it might be a reality show. In any case the harbormaster accepted the coins in payment for dockage and compensation for Petros. He adjourned to his station on the other side of the harbor with a wild story to tell and re-tell during the winter nights ahead when port arrivals were few and far between.

The crew meanwhile asked the archaeologist where they could

eat and were directed to Kounela's Fish Restaurant. They invited the archaeologist along as interpreter and brought the carcass of Petros, which they insisted on roasting with the fish.

They feasted and drank into the late afternoon. They were notably uncouth and failed to use the cutlery provided. Instead they unsheathed their bronze knives to debone the fish and ate with their fingers. Some crewman slyly put the cheap tin spoons and forks into their pouches thinking they were made of silver. The waiters were fearful of them because of their extreme lack of manners – spitting on the floor and carving designs in the tables and said nothing as some of them napped after dinner on the floor using quivers full of arrows as pillows. The owner of the restaurant was more than happy to oblige their wishes for more wine and more fish when he was presented with a handful of rare ancient coins. He was no expert but even if they were not real he could display them in his fish tank. He was also in no mood for confrontation.

By now my friend was taking notes. He was invited on board the ship and was asked where a good careenage could be found. He knew that ancient mariners normally drew their ships up onto land at night so he suggested Elia Beach on the south side of Mykonos. To show them where exactly they took him along. He marveled at their salt-encrusted purple sail when it was unfurled to catch the wind. As they maneuvered the vessel, sailors to the beat of a drum splashed their oars in unison. It was twilight when they hove to on Elia Beach and scraped their boat up onto the sand.

Although the Elia taverna was packed during beach-going hours, now it was occupied by just a few romantic couples supping by candlelight and the tunes of light jazz. Their idyll was interrupted by the ruckus of men hacking apart straw beach umbrellas and wooden beach chairs. They piled them up and lit a huge bonfire.

Having stolen a mound of provisions at Kounela's they were soon feasting and drinking retsina wine from the huge rubber containers fishermen favored then. And what would be a party without women? Many adventurous female tourists after seeing movies featuring Greek Lotharios were attracted to the island by the plethora of attractive men but found out later they were mostly gay. This created a level of desire that gibed with the bearded newcomers who seemed to be heterosexual on steroids. Several women seeing the fire came over from a nearby hotel. Soon more showed up alerted by cellphone calls from the others.

By the time the police arrived, called by Nikos the taverna owner when his bar was about to be pillaged, the beach party had turned into a full-fledged orgy. Since no one could speak to any other, it was a matter of winks and nudges that advanced to stronger gestures. The archaeologist would later write a paper on the universality through history of gesture as expressed on Greek vases. He could not, of course, reveal what sparked his interest or some of his knowledge as the Argonauts used their fingers as semaphores to communicate to each other.

A few of the women had retreated to dark corners and were deep in the throes of sex. Later some would say it was indeed an experience to couple with unwashed beasts but wouldn't want to repeat it. Others disappeared after the arrows began to fly.

Ultimately the police prevailed when the archers exhausted their quivers. Fortunately they were so drunk that none of their arrows had hit their marks. The police called for reinforcements and moved in to try to arrest the vandals of the beach furniture. Someone on the force started a rumor that the ship had to be an elaborate cover for smuggling drugs.

When they had subdued the crew who were feeling no pain anyway, they searched through some seamen's bags and found nothing but oddities – at least to the police. In truth it was loot in forms we don't particularly value these days – yards of silk, metal objects of unknown utility, seashells and tiny pieces of amber, cutlery from their afternoon repast.

In the captain's quarters on board the ship they found a bag larger than the others. It was tied around with heavy rope and the police instinctively surmised this had to be the mother lode. It was, but not in the way they thought: it was filled with air, to be precise the *meltemi* the sailors told them through their archaeologist translator– the cold north wind that blows out of the Balkans, often like a gale.

The captain and his crew took advantage of the disarray caused by the wind whooshing out of its unbound container. It blew harder than anyone on Mykonos could remember, sandblasted the police and heaved the black ship with its painted eye off the shore and into the water. Even their sail was not necessary as the ship with the help of its oars was steered straight out to sea. It was last seen by a cruise liner out of Rhodes in the straits between Mykonos and Naxos heading south.

The archaeologist and the police picked through the scene the next morning before the beachgoers arrived. They gathered the arrows, several bronze axes, some coins, an armored helmet and a few other items strewn around. These were shipped to the lab attached to the archaeological museum in Athens. The report that came back insisted the items all dated to about 500 BC. With no leads and for a small bribe from the archaeologist the police suppressed the report by misfiling it. The archaeologist would have lost his professional credentials if he revealed all he knew.

THE BLACK CAIQUE

One windy day Angelos and I sat at a café on the waterfront awaiting our espressos. No cruise ship was in port that morning so the passerby were either locals, like housewives in black fingering fish at the market by the shore in front of us, or lightly clad tourists heading towards beaches but stopping on the way to photograph Mykonos' mascot, Petros the Pelican. Angelos eyes turned to a gazelle-like beauty with just a sarong covering her bikini.

"When I was young I'd run after her and offer a coffee. Now I admire from a distance. A lot easier," Angelos remarked.

"I miss the adventure," I said. "Any day I hoped to meet the love of my life."

Just as our espressos arrived so did a man of about our age guided by an attractive younger woman. He tapped tapped his white cane and sat down at the table next to us.

"Nathan, I haven't seen you for forever," Angelos said. The man smiled from behind his sunglasses.

"Living in the boondocks, I don't get to town much," Nathan said with an American accent. "Gretel's mother has been ill and she's had to take care of all of us," he said pointing to his companion.

After we were introduced I asked Nathan how he came to live on Mykonos.

"Would you like to hear why? I have the time but do you?" Nathan asked.

"The greatest storytellers are blind. Remember Homer," Angelos said. "Of course we do!" Nathan smiled but I don't think he meant it.

I was a writer in my late twenties when I arrived in Mykonos forty years ago. The first novel of Nathan Strong had just been published to sparse reviews and fewer sales – a campus romance at my alma mater. It was what is called literary, meaning there were no murders, some fancy description (of Smith girls), and a few experiments with form—I called the chapters "cantos" and kept them short.

Lawrence Durrell had just published a book about his extensive travels through the Greek Islands and like him I was infected with an inordinate love for those specks of land in the Aegean Sea the Venetians called the Archipelago. Other islands had their virtues – Patmos was quiet, Samos pine-scented and airy – but Mykonos filled the bill for me. At that time the tourist boom had not yet begun in earnest – out-of-the-way places could be found to write - and there was a continual supply of willing girls (and boys) arriving every day.

I was as free as only the young and healthy can be, enough money in my pocket for a summer, and the first pages of my second book down on paper.

I took a room in a private dwelling in the port (there were few hotels then), wrote mornings, and socialized afternoons on the beach. Those outside of town were still pristine before caiques and buses from the port began to arrive in later years. Most had a taverna or two tucked away behind them, but none were plagued by the ubiquitous umbrellas and chairs that cover the sands now.

When I arrived in June I managed to neatly bisect my day, but by the time July rolled around, what happened at night began to interfere. Hours on Mykonos were late – no one sat down to dinner before ten or eleven, and the bars and discos beckoned after that. As a result I rarely tucked in before the wee hours and sometimes greeted the dawn the wrong way around. Then there were the girls. You never knew when you'd be in luck, or were simply wasting time. When I managed to find a compliant one, it was usually for just a week or two – vacationers were here for shorter periods than me. All of this slowed down my writing, and since I had not yet found my living muse, I became depressed in what everyone else considered paradise.

One day, to vary what had become routine, a few of us chartered a caique and invited some nice looking new arrivals to picnic with us on Rhenia, a neighboring and deserted island. In ancient times it was the burial ground for the city on Delos, just across a narrow strait. Delos had been declared sacred – it was known as the birth place of Apollo and Artemis – so mortals could not be born or die there.

The wonderfully named Kosta Charon owned the boat, which unlike the others painted in Matisse-y reds, yellows and blues was a distinctive black. He was dark himself, oak-colored leathery skin and a Stalin-like moustache and so weather-beaten he looked sixty but probably was younger.

We spent a frolicksome day lying on a beach whose pebbles were interspersed with potshards rounded with age, swam in waters over strange architectural shapes below – column drums and architraves – and though I had not seen him angling, ate a lunch Kosta prepared of a giant fish he said was freshly caught. Dessert was watermelon. Since we were all naked and crowded into the cabin of his boat, we ended up dribbled in pink with watermelon seeds sticking in our pubic hair. A large drum of retsina wine fueled our revels and later siestas basking in the sun.

The day had been windstill and hot, but as the sun descended in late afternoon what's locally known as the *meltemi*—the strong north wind that blows out of the Balkans—whipped up whitecaps. We were in good spirits as we stumbled back onto Kosta's bobbing boat.

"Don't worry about the waves," Kosta said, and before he took the rudder, he raised his arms to heaven and let loose a bellow that would have been impressive even on the stage of the Metropolitan Opera - his way of saying, "*All aboard*," – the other boatmen used horns or blew through a conch shell.

Was it coincidence that the wind changed direction, the sea calmed and we putt-putted back the four or five miles to Mykonos, sailing through soup? I sat next to the rudder with Kosta, and asked him if he had always lived in Mykonos. "Most of the time" he said in fluent English he told me he had picked up working for several years in a Greek diner in Moline, Illinois. "I fish for tourists in summer, for myself the rest of the year. "See those fields over there" he said as we rounded a promontory next to unexcavated ruins of Delos. "They've never been touched by archaeologists. In winter, I'm sometimes stranded and I've found wonderful things."

I know it is forbidden to privately dig and abscond with artifacts but I couldn't resist asking, "What kind of things?" "Wonderful things," he repeated.

"Why do you think my boat is painted black? There's no moon for the next few days. If you like I'll take you there tomorrow. After the sun goes down." He turned and put his arm around an attractive dark girl I had no recollection of seeing before. "Maybe my little Gretchen would like to go too," he said and grinned, baring his perfect white teeth.

Putting aside any ethical qualms I paid him the paltry drachmas he asked for the next evening's adventure, and soon we were on our way. His little Gretchen was on board, too, sleeping below. At one point we saw faint lights on small fishing boats in the distance. I heard a muffled blast. Startled, I stood up.

"Don't worry. Lights attract the fish and dynamite brings up a lot of dead ones. That's why it's illegal."

Instead of rounding the north edge of Delos as we had the day before, we approached around the southern tip of the island and anchored just offshore from what Kosta told me was the Aesclepion – the ancient hospital where illnesses were cured by special dreams, under the supervision of priests. "Snakes were involved. They were considered sacred healers. To this day the symbol for medicine remains a wand with two intertwined serpents." Kosta seemed to know more than the typical boatman.

We waded knee-deep into the water and onto the beach and sat for a time on smooth marble slabs that still retained warmth from the day. Kosta was in a talkative mood but Gretchen seemed drugged. She yawned, stretched and fell asleep again. "Let her rest," he said as he grabbed two combat shovels, made for scooping out foxholes, and beckoned me to follow.

"There are guards here but very few. You can see them coming. They use flashlights so they won't step on the snakes." He laughed.

"What about us?"

"Don't worry, I know how to talk to them." I wondered if he meant the guards, or the snakes.

"Here is a good spot," Kosta announced and began digging in the earth slowly and as quietly as he could. To illuminate his progress I held his cigarette lighter close to the ground. In a few minutes lo and behold appeared the glint of metal.

"Look a coin. Only bronze but old. See the palm tree on this side? That's the one under which Leto bore Apollo and Artemis." Scraping dirt from it he pointed out a lyre on the reverse that symbolized Apollo. Soon after we found a cylindrical piece of ivory which Kosta said was part of a flute shepherds played.

"Not so old," he said. We dug around for an hour or so but found nothing more.

I had caught the treasure hunting bug but Kosta said we should go back to Mykonos since light would soon be returning to the skies. He snapped his fingers when we returned to Gretchen still asleep on her marble, and she awoke, rubbed her eyes, and smiled. I wondered about her relation to Kosta? She fell asleep again as we were underway. Kosta held the rudder with his foot and I sat beside him on a night silent except for the putt putt of his boat and marveled at a sky filled with more stars than I had ever seen.

I told Kosta that the coincidences that happened around him seemed like magic. The big fish, calming the wind, finding the coin so quickly.

"You must be in tune with the universe. That is my secret. How to do it? That is something else. Maybe one day I'll teach you."

"Black magic?" I joked. He didn't answer.

As dawn began to spread its rosy fingers over the Aegean, I disembarked at the harbor and watched Kosta with his sleeping girl below sail off to wherever he lived.

I slept late with strange dreams and woke up sweating in direct sunlight since I had forgotten to close my shutters. After a very late breakfast I sat down to write. I had been working on a theme of an expatriate American in Paris, remembering my junior year of college there, but it all seemed so banal. Henry James to Hemingway to James Jones – it had been done. What could I offer that was different? That I was homesick at first and took up reading Sinclair Lewis and Thomas Wolfe? That Cole Porter and Picasso were no longer around? That I played hookey watching Brigitte Bardot flicks on afternoons I was supposed to be in class?

The more I thought about it the more I wanted to know about Kosta, but he seemed to have disappeared. Someone told me they heard he had gone to Patmos for religious reasons. Other boatmen I asked were evasive. Perhaps he was hired for a private trip to Tinos or Paros, they offered.

For a week I suffered from writer's block. That year in Paris seemed further away than ever. My mood didn't help me with women either. Once my heart leaped when I thought I saw Gretchen in the white labyrinth of streets behind the port but it proved to be someone else. I even dreamed I disrobed her in the boat and found magic spells tattooed on her torso.

Kosta returned nine days after our nocturnal voyage, hale and hearty. He greeted me with a high five. I told him of my travails and he said in a low voice, "I have a solution to your problem. See me at Kamare's café on the port at eleven tonight." After he left I realized that I never asked him where he had been or what he had been up to.

I arrived on time and found him conversing with a bald man wearing thick black rimmed glasses. "This is Vladimir. He is my lawyer," he said by way of introduction. After I sat down the two ignored me as they continued their talk (accompanied by hand signals) in rapid fire Greek. Bored, I watched a giant ferry from Pireaus enter the harbor at speed and rotate 180 degrees as smartly as if it were a Porsche positioning itself for docking. Kosta ordered a round of ouzos and when we finished, Vlad the lawyer flourished a legal document. It stated Kosta would teach me what he knew, help me to prosper and in general grease my way through the world for twenty-nine years or one circuit of Saturn though an astrological chart. In return he would own my soul.

"You've got to be kidding," I said after scanning the document. "I'm Faust and you are Mephistopheles right?"

"Who?" The lawyer asked in a way that seemed honest. Kosta had stolen Goethe's plot but claimed to know nothing of *Faust*. *It's the exact same story*, I thought but these two bumpkins imagine they've made it up.

"What do you intend to do with my soul?" I asked Vladimir with tongue in cheek.

"Whatever Kosta wants. The future is unknowable," the lawyer said.

"If it is unknowable how can you be sure Kosta will get it in twenty-nine years."

"Details. Details," Vladimir said as if I were nitpicking.

"O.K. I'll sign," I said, out of curiosity more than anything else.

If by a slight chance they were right, I reasoned Kosta would surely be buried by then. After a pep talk telling me what he would do for me, I was nearly convinced. He then mentioned that I would have to humor Gretchen, whom he called his assistant, by sleeping with her. "Your seed will seal the deal." This would not be a problem for me.

"What happens after twenty-nine years? Do I die?" I asked as a joke.

"Not necessarily. To be honest you might not like what may happen."

"I guess I have to take my chances," I said with a jaunty tone.

When we dispersed into the night I could barely believe what had happened. Were they nuts? They appeared to be deadly serious. The least that could transpire was that I would get a chance to sleep with silent Gretchen; the most that I would receive everything I desired. Not a bad deal overall. Why did they choose me? *Why not?* my ego replied. *You are young, talented, intelligent.* Was the spell already working?

Kosta disappeared, but Gretchen showed up at my door in the wee hours two days later. After I let her in wordlessly she shimmied out of her dress. She lay down on my bed, raised her arms, and clasped her hands – an intimate gesture that showed me her body was mine. After a tentative start we made silent, groping love for what seemed like hours. I couldn't get enough of her musky smell. When we finished I was infatuated.

"Can we meet again?" I asked.

She did not answer but enigmatically put her finger to her lips and dressed. As she slipped away I yelled after her. "Where can I find you?" There was no answer. I wondered if it was a language issue. The next day I walked the town searching and asking for Kosta and her. No one knew a Gretchen nor again where Kosta was. It was fruitless.

One June day decades later I directed the skipper of my chartered yacht to aim towards Mykonos for the first time since my success. Maybe a return visit would jar me out of the professional rut I found myself in. I had made my fortune on thrillers, which almost like magic became bestsellers - some were even made into films. Now I wanted to probe deeper and become a serious author like those that used to be pictured on Barnes and Noble bags. Dickens. Shakespeare. Dostoyevsky. And why not? I remembered my happy summer there. The simple white-washed lanes and houses. Early mornings in the port watching farmers on donkeys selling flowers and vegetables. The boat that carried us back and forth to the beaches in sparkling sunshine. The *passagietta* of residents and visitors alike as dusk fell, the round of the bars and discos at night.

The first thing I noticed as we docked at a new marina outside of town were three large cruise liners – the kind that carry thousands of passengers and another thousand in crew. The next thing I saw was that my yacht was no longer large. One

131

moored next to us flying a Saudi flag even sported gold-plated fittings. Before when cars had to be winched individually from holds of cargo ships they were rare on the island. When ferries modeled after navy landing craft made their appearance, the clop of livestock and human feet was replaced by a cacaphony of scooters, cycles, autos and trucks.

I was disoriented as I strolled the lanes. I remembered their meanders but now the sandal makers and grocery stores had been replaced with shops bearing the names of Hermes, Vuitton, Cartier—just like Cannes or Beverly Hills. Signs directed visitors to swanky restaurants in hidden gardens. Streets nearer the port hosted souvenir shops and jewelers of low-end bling catering to denizens of the cruise boats. It seemed every European tramway conductor was in town with his family. Even the formerly matte lime-based whitewash on the streets and walls that was renewed weekly had given way to shiny longer lasting paint.

In the old days there was one elegant restaurant, Katrine's hidden in the back streets. At the time it was the only one on the island that served lettuce wondrously brought from Athens. Then it was too expensive except for passing shipowners although once I splurged there with a Swedish beauty I was trying to impress. Miraculously it was still in business and I sat down with several of my yachting guests to dine on imported Dover sole and bottles of cold Chassagne-Montrachet. Halfway through I thought I saw Kosta Charon pass by with a non-Greek looking woman in her mid-twenties. Of course it wasn't him. He could not appear unchanged after twenty-eight years. Mykonos men aged poorly – their faces were seamed and wrinkled by the sea and hard winters before they were forty. Still, it made me recall that time with his so-called lawyer. I wasn't so superstitious as to believe anything I agreed to then could be operative today and I told my guests the story which elicited much hilarity. Just to flip off any incipient fear, after dinner I directed our walk to the same café where the deal had been consummated so long ago. I regaled them with stories of what it was like to live in Mykonos before it was "discovered." Being my guests, they laughed at the right places and asked questions that revealed how erudite they themselves were. We were tipsy as midnight approached and the man that looked like Kosta with his girl passed by again but then stopped.

"Remember me?" he asked and stretched out his arms. The booming voice was the same. Of course I remembered but I hesitated, pretending I needed time to recollect.

"Ah yes, Kosta," I said and we embraced. "Kosta," I said to my guests, "had the most elegant caique in Mykonos; the only one painted black." I winked at them so they would know who he was. "Who is the beauty you are with?"

"She is the new Gretchen. Her name is Gretel," he said with a wide mustachioed grin that displayed his perfect set of teeth.

Gretel did indeed look like Gretchen, not blonde but lighter than Gretchen's dark beauty. Could she be her daughter?

"Where is Hansel?" one of my guests asked.

Kosta shot him a hard glance. I gave him another wink.

"Whatever happened to Gretchen?" I asked Kosta.

"That is a long story, best left to another time. I know your yacht. I will come and visit you tomorrow," Kosta said matter-of-factly as if he had been invited.

You can imagine all the memories that snaked through my head, even if they were dulled by alcohol and time. What remained sharp, however, was a long-buried dread suddenly uncovered– of a confrontation I knew might happen.

The black caique appeared the next morning next to our berth, its mast barely reaching the upper deck of my vessel. I directed my sailors to allow Kosta to board. He was alone and I invited him to sit on the aft deck under a striped awning. A steward brought coffee and fruit. After the usual pleasantries I tried to deflect the inevitable by asking Kosta about Gretchen.

"She is alive, pretty old now. She was in a terrible accident after you left. That was her daughter last night if you haven't figured it out."

"Gretel does look like her," I observed.

Kosta put up his wide palm, like a stop sign. "Let us not beat around the bush. If you remember, we made a deal with a due date coming up. I want to collect on it."

I laughed a strangled laugh. "I never considered it serious. You were joking with me – that talk of my seed and all?"

"Why would I bring a lawyer to a meeting that was not serious?" Kosta replied. "I gave you what you have become. Now I want back what is mine."

I saw by the scowl on his face and his posture, holding the arms of the chair like a tiger ready to pounce that he was indeed serious. Suddenly he relaxed and in the most friendly tone said we should go see Gretchen and her daughter who lived in the countryside near the inland village of Ano Mera. "However, you must come alone with me. She is not well and cannot take too much company."

After a swift taxi ride on the paved highway that had replaced the old winding road (itself a notch above the donkey path it had been) and dodging traffic heading for the beaches, we arrived at a dingy house in a cul-de-sac. Kosta knocked and the young Gretel appeared at the door barefoot with tangled hair and a flowered smock. She was prettier than I had remembered from the day before. In a naïve way she examined me head to toe.

"Mama," she called. I did not at first recognize her as Gretchen hunched out of the shuttered gloom covered in black, her face veiled like a Moslem in a burka.

"Do you remember my friend?" Kosta asked her. She nodded. Slowly she lifted her veil and I gasped. Disfigured, she grinned. She was a figure out of a nightmare. I could just (barely) see a resemblance to the radiant Gretchen I had constructed in my daydreams over the years.

"What happened to her?" I asked Kosta.

"You know she has always been mute." I didn't, I had assumed she couldn't speak English. "She tried to leave the island when her daughter was a baby without telling me. No one knows why but acid was thrown in her face and over her breasts. I don't know what came over her. But good comes from bad. Look at her daughter. Just like mother. Maybe even more beautiful. Unlike her mother, this one can talk. Speak to the man," Kosta ordered.

"Welcome to our home," she said in broken English, her eyes downcast.

The young Gretel prepared tea in glass mugs for us. Kosta motioned for me to sit down next to him in what passed for a garden in front of the house.

"What kind of new deal would you go for, Kosta," I asked, "to extend our agreement?" I would humor him with all the syrupy wheedling I had observed in years of dealing with agents, promoters, and producers. "I'm sure I have what you want and I can give it to you."

"If I wanted riches, money, I could find it myself. I'm a simple man. All I need is for my boat and my friends." *And fancy chompers*, I added to myself. "And your soul."

"What would you do with it?" I asked. "What could it be worth? With some of my money you can buy an ocean of souls. I bet you could buy them cheap in some place like Libya."

"Don't toy with me," Kosta said. "It is about particular souls at particular times. That is what keeps me alive," he said and laughed. "Think it over. By the way, Gretel is your daughter as I imagine you have already figured out."

When Gretel returned I examined her as she had me. Could it be? My only progeny. I'm on a yacht. She's in a hovel. It was similar to the beginning of a plot of one of my novels.

"Can I kiss her goodbye?" I asked as we prepared to leave. I embraced her. She misunderstood and rubbed her young body against me as a whore would, soliciting business.

"What would you actually want me to do if you owned my soul?" I asked Kosta on the way back to the port.

"It is too late. I already own it. Perhaps I might test you by having you break Gretel's arms or sleep with her," He laughed. "I'm just kidding. Whatever I want, Voodoo? You will be my American zombie." He laughed again. "You have a few weeks left."

The dreams and plans for the next chapters of my life were lined-up in my mind like scenes in a long opera. Now everything was jumbled. Even though I found it hard to believe his preposterous ideas how could I cajole Kosta into making a new deal just in case? I needed time to write my new and serious books. My opus, if I stopped now, would consist of a series of trashy novels. And what responsibility did I have for Gretel?

My yacht stayed in port that week with much coming and going. I even consulted a lawyer in New York who thought I was crazy to even consider an agreement like this a contract. He suggested I hire security guards. I examined ways I could kidnap Gretel. In the end I decided my imagination, fueled as it was with the thrillers I'd written, was getting away from me and I decided Kosta was just an ultimately harmless, old fraud, and anyway he seemed to have disappeared.

One evening as I stepped from my teak-decked launch onto the town dock, an old woman dressed all in black and wearing a kerchief that hid most of her face approached with her hand out. Assuming she was a beggar I searched my pocket for a few coins and offered them to her. Instead she uncapped a vial held in her other hand and splashed its contents which later proved to be acid in my face. The crone scuttling away was the last thing I would ever see.

The local police after a desultory search for the poisoner

decided she was most likely demented. She could be anyone they said-all the *yia yias* here look the same. And what could be her motive?

The best doctors could not save my sight. I was helicoptered first to Athens and then jetted to Zurich to a special eye clinic. I did not reveal my suspicions of Kosta to them. It was too unbelievable.

Everything, surprisingly did not end badly. In the months I was in Zurich one of the doctors with whom I became intimate pointed out how my story resonated with Goethe's *Faust*. Apparently, the great C.J. Jung himself considered the Faust legend in all its permutations a linchpin of Western Civilization – that constant but never satisfied striving and longing for what could be – the attitude that had built modern science and industry at the expense of the soul. He inspired me to establish a charitable foundation, which he would run of course.

I kept just enough money to enable me to live and support Gretchen and Gretel. Their hovel became my home after I paid to fix it up. Just as the blind Milton dictated *Paradise Lost* to his daughter, I dictated the story of my life (lightly fictionalized) to Gretel here. She has never married.

I realized the contract was marked paid when I heard while convalescing in Switzerland that Kosta's black caique was found drifting off Delos with his badly decomposed body still at the helm. The yachtsman who found it had a classical bent and said it reminded him of Charon's boat on the River Styx.

Nathan's tale went on so long that we ended up paying for his and Gretel's lunch. After they left we drank the afternoon away weighing what would be the pros and cons of meeting our own Mephistopheles.

JUDGMENT OF PARIS

"One of the things I love about Mykonos is that modern life here so often resonates with venerable tales," I said. "When a caique comes into port there is Odysseus hurling down the anchor. After a few old salts imbibe too much retsina wine they link arms and step to the ancient crane dance." Angelos raised his glass of ouzo. As if in answer a rough sea lightly sprayed us through the Kastro Bar's window. "That reminds me of a tale an archaeologist friend told me that affected him deeply because it was such a close parallel to the classical story of the Judgment of Paris," Angelos said. "You remember how Paris is asked to choose the best of a trio of goddesses. Hera brings power, Athena prowess in battle and Aphrodite beauty in the form of the most ravishing woman ever-Helen of Troy." Bear in mind that during the nineteenth century the major archaeological sites in Greece were apportioned out to various nationalities. There was a two-fold benefit –bribes and jobs for the locals and their rulers, and cementing diplomatic ties in Athens. The Americans still retain the Athenian Agora concession to this day; the Germans have Olympia; the British, Knossos; and the French have exclusive rights for excavating in two major places dedicated to Apollo – Delphi and Delos. So it has come to pass that the sole current inhabitants of our neighboring island the ancient classical city of Delos and the birth place of the sacred twins, Apollo and Artemis, are the guards and French archaeologists who live in houses near the old harbor.

It is a Spartan existence. One of the scientists grandly named Louis de Dampierre was my drinking companion on the port one evening. He was spending a day or two of R and R here on Mykonos a few miles across the water from his Delian exile. As we savored the maidens sauntering by, baring as much of their skin as they possibly could, he complained about the lack of same on Delos, except once.

"As it happened a colleague of mine Alexandre de Rubempre stepped outside his bungalow one morning to take a swim before the day's work began—sure to be hot and sweaty, scrabbling in the dirt of centuries as always," Louis began. "It was also before the first tourist boats from Mykonos were scheduled to arrive, and he expected to be alone as he plunged into the warm Aegean *sans maillot*. When Alexandre completed his laps he walked out of the sea and found himself full frontal to three young women sitting on the strand."

"*Bonjour*," he said gallantly as he wrapped a towel around his midriff. They did not appear shocked. "Where do you come from?"

"We are from Athens," one of the girls said, in an accent that broadcast Oxford.

"How do you speak such perfect English?"

"We're on summer break now but we study in England," replied Hera.

"We swam from Hera's father's yacht. You see it over there off Rhenia," said Athena. Rhenia, formerly the cemetery for Delos, is an island just yards away.

You might surmise by now the third girl was named Aphrodite. Alexandre found it charming – the classical names lived on - Socrates was one of his foremen at their dig. He rarely ran across French men named Clovis or Vercingetorix.

He was even more charmed by their beauty and skimpy bikinis, and invited them into his simple digs for coffee.

Not only were they beautiful, they were intelligent – a rare combination he found. Hera confided that she wanted to be an archaeologist herself, but was struggling with her father who had other plans, like marrying dynastically. Athena said she loved gymnastics –her dream was to represent Greece in the Olympics one day. Aphrodite, airier than the other two spoke of her poetry.

"If you act nice you might be the subject of one," she said to Alexandre, batting her liquid eyes.

All this time, he was trying to figure out how he could manage to keep in touch with these lovelies when he went to work. His worries were pre-empted when Hera asked him to dine with them on the yacht that evening. "My father should meet a bona fide archaeologist" she said.

I have studied neo-Platonism among other philosophies, and I have a strong sense that one's destiny is determined by the interaction of your personal *daemon,* (or guardian angel as it is more commonly put nowadays) with one's free will and overarching fate. That's why I thought it was not such a coincidence when Alexandre's boss chose that very morning to ask him if he would mind travelling to the Temple of Apollo at Didyma, a short distance from the ancient Ionian city of Miletus in present-day Turkey. In antiquity an oracle almost as famous as the one in Delphi resided there. A German archaeologist had discovered marble tablets that implied some kind of link with Delos, which Alexandre's boss wanted to pursue. "You can leave tomorrow."

That evening Alexandre dined as scheduled on the yacht after a bumpy ride on his Zodiac rubber boat. The *meltemi* was blowing and even the large vessel rocked in the precipitation-less tempest. Except for Hera's rather dour father and mother, Dimitri and Kassandra, Alexandre was in heaven as the three women catered to him, each trying to outdo the others. Dimitri was impressed that Alexandre possessed titled relatives.

When Alexandre announced he must leave the next day, Papa Dimitri grandly offered to take him there. The girls clamored to go too. They had never been. Would Alexandre mind?

"We can share expenses," said Hera.

And so we find my handsome friend along with three even more handsome girls driving a rutted road through Ionia. He nearly lost the women when he stopped for gas near the ruins of Priene. The filling station attendant, whose teeth were split evenly between stumps and metal, was so intent on ogling the women that he overfilled the tank. Fortunately, the cigarette that dangled from his lips was not lit.

By late afternoon they had crossed the delta of the Maeander River, now a silted plain covered with tall grassy reeds. Even Alexandre himself was not prepared for the grandeur of Apollo's temple. Only three pillars were left looming atop a high staircase but they were taller than any he had seen from antiquity. Legend had it that the temple precinct behind was so vast that its architects could not manage to roof it. Now it was an outdoor space as large as a ball field.

The bearded German archaeologist in charge was found living nearby in a small colony of tents. "I did not know you would bring assistants. But, um, we have extra sleeping bags."

Alexandre did not disabuse the German of his notion. They looked the role, if perhaps too perfectly—magazine fantasies of archaeologists dressed in tailored khaki, and wearing pith helmets and laced-up boots.

That night the new arrivals dined with Kurt the German at a restaurant in the small village that had grown up around the temple's ruins. They washed it down with raki, the Turkish version of ouzo, and were more than merry. In fact you might say the women were becoming amorous. Kurt was stiff as a nail and making little headway since Alexandre, being French like me, held all the cards. The mood sustained itself when they repaired to their tent. With much laughter and by the light of a candle, they undressed half-in, half-out of their sleeping bags.

"What if we were the three graces? Which one of us would you choose?" Hera asked.

"That is a loaded question. Why don't I say all of you," replied Alexandre.

"All at once or separately?" Athena asked with a laugh, awaiting his reaction.

Diplomatically, Alexandre suggested they should sleep on it.

In the morning he met with Kurt in his office in a ramshackle building the Germans had bought next to the temple, the women in tow to keep up appearances. Kurt uncovered a plaque that had been discovered a week before. "Alexandre later told me what it said in eroded but readable marble letters. A Sybil was sent from Didyma to establish an oracle in Delos. It suggests she brought an important gift with her. As you may know Didyma possessed one of the most important oracles in classical times. Delos had one, too, but it was not so important. Delphi and Didyma were the major leagues for Apollo's oracles – remember he was among other things the god of prophecy.

"What my colleagues and I want to know," asked Kurt, "is if you have any evidence that would tie in with our sibyl being set up as an oracle in Delos. And what was the gift? We think it might have been a golden arrow, but it might just refer to her."

All the time Kurt was talking and while they leaned over the inscribed plaque, Aphrodite was rubbing Alexandre's ankle up and down gently with her boot. Alexandre didn't mind.

Kurt, also with hope for a break from his bachelor's existence arranged a lunchtime picnic among some unexcavated ruins beneath gently swelling hills nearby. *It is like a dream of paradise*, Alexandre thought, as they lolled on Turkish carpets like pashas, drinking wine and eating red tomatoes, purple grapes, and white goat cheese spread on toasty pita bread baked that very morning. A slight breeze picked up and lightened the heat of the sun that dappled their dining area, carpeted with pine needles through the shade of trees. Alexandre thought of Botticelli's *Primavera*, his favorite painting. It portrayed the same mood they were surrounded by here, a quiet time out of which magic might spring.

After their repast most dozed off, Athena baring an artfully revealed breast falling out of her loose chemise; her arms behind her head and legs akimbo as if she were ready for Pan. Aphrodite whose desire to win was stronger than her friends arose when the coast was clear and beckoned Alexandre to follow her behind a stand of oleander bushes next to their picnic place. She attacked him with a kiss and pulled him to the ground. She was nude under her khaki shirt and shorts. She squeezed the front of his pants and found that he was responsive. They made love in the grass as silently as they could. In response to a question from one of the others when they returned, Aphrodite said they had enjoyed a short stroll. Athena who asked the question smirked. Hera looked pissed. Alexandre figured it was because of his charm. As in the judgment of Paris, Aphrodite had won. She was the most beautiful of the three, Alexandre thought, but in the fable Aphrodite had offered Helen of Troy, not herself.

Later after a sweltering day scrambling around the excavations and seeing what relics had already been found, Alexandre pulled Aphrodite aside and asked when they could do it again. To his surprise, he was turned down.

"Haven't you figured it out yet?" Aphrodite said with a big grin on her face. "We are all lesbians. We were playing a game with you and I won." After Aphrodite had let the cat out of the bag, his trio of "assistants" felt free to snuggle together like a litter of kittens the next night. Alexandre prided himself on being able to accept anything, but it was disquieting that he had missed any sign of the girls sexual bent. And he was horny.

This too would be assuaged the following evening next to the great temple of Apollo Didymus. A banquet was laid out daringly inside the temple's grassy precinct where a lamb roasted on a spit. After the feast Kurt provided entertainment in the form of a dusky gypsy-like girl who danced for them in flouncy petticoats and a bare midriff.

Alexandre was enthralled by the antiquity of it all – the harmonica accompaniment which he likened to Pan's pipes, the castanets, like ancient rattles called sistrums which he had only seen before in museums.

Afterwards an old lady sidled up to Alexandre. "You like her?" she said pointing to the dancer at her side. At first Alexandre thought the old woman was asking for a tip, and he reached into his pocket. "No monsieur, it is not necessary. You like her for, you know, love? No money. Come," she said.

Alexandre who originally had the woman pegged as the gypsy's mother now decided she might be her procurer but found it odd she demanded no baksheesh. Dutifully led by his desire, Alexandre followed the women into a lean-to built against a side of the stone wall that enclosed the temple. The girl smiled shyly and said her name was Cumae.

"Like the sybil? The famous sybil of Cumae loved by Apollo?" Alexandre asked.

"What is sibyl?" asked Cumae.

The old woman disappeared and Alexandre with rising interest watched the girl detach her bra-like top and slip out of her petticoats. All she wore now were earrings, nose and navel rings, and dangling bracelets on her wrists and ankles. Her nipples were erect as she rubbed her body against his. She pulled him down onto a pile of pelts of sheep, made more luxuriant and barbaric by what appeared to be the hides of a lion and a leopard.

Cumae glowed as they lay next to each other afterwards glistening with sweat. She was not as conventionally beautiful as Aphrodite but she had soul. Alexandre felt a pang that could be love. She was uneducated – her desire to please him during lovemaking told him that. Frenchwomen are sexy but demanding – touch me like this, lick me here. They considered themselves equal to a man. How nice it was to have a love slave!

By now Cumae had dressed. To show his appreciation Alexandre pressed some Turkish lira notes into her palm but she seemed offended and pushed them away. The old woman trundled back as Alexandre tried to make clear that he wanted to meet Cumae again.

"Tomorrow is my last day here. I must see you."

The woman answered for her by saying "no, no" wagging her finger. "One time only," she said. It was becoming a pattern. "Why?"

"She is Cumae," the old woman said.

What kind of answer is that? thought Alexandre. He decided to be firmer. "I will see you tomorrow at nine o'clock." He tapped his watch. "Be there," he said. They both smiled as he left for his tent and the three unavailable goddesses eager for news and with some of their own.

"Guess what Kurt told Hera after Alexandre left?" Louis said. "The old lady *is* the young girl's mother. She is a fortune teller and is training her daughter to be one too. This is the interesting part. Kurt said there is a folk tradition around Didyma of a matriarchal line of fortune tellers that goes back as far as anyone remembers. Each generation begets a girl to continue in an unbroken line. The fathers are selected by the mothers. The spirits tell them when the right guy comes along to do stud duty." The girls laughed. "Did you sleep with her?" Alexandre blushed.

"I guess you were it."

Cumae and her mother did not show up nor were they to be found anywhere the next morning. Before their final leave-taking Alexandre waited for Kurt to be alone to ask a few questions.

"It may be even older," Kurt said. Some of us have speculated that the tradition harks back to the time when Apollo's oracle was resident here. You know the girl's name Cumae is not a Turkish one. And you've heard of the sibyl of Cumae. And you know sibyls were prophetesses. Put it all together and add this interesting fact. The lean-to where Cumae and her mother live is the only dwelling place allowed by the locals so close to their prime tourist attraction. When I mentioned we should force them to move elsewhere they refused to be involved."

Alexandre wanted to know more but his "assistants" clamored to get going. They had at least three hours of rough roads to Kusadasi until the one boat a day to Samos sailed. Papa would be waiting there on his white yacht.

On the passage back to Delos to drop Alexandre off, the girls teased him unmercifully about his new peasant girlfriend. "She's no Helen of Troy," Aphrodite said.

In later years the "goddesses" all made good marriages by Greek shipowner standards and their mutual secret was kept. Alexandre kept his secret too. Because of the Didyma plaque he turned up new evidence about the heretofore little known oracle of Delos. That inspired him to do research on the place of oracles and oracular sybils in ancient Greece. He became not only one of the world's experts on the subject but the progeniture of one of them.

A Kouros

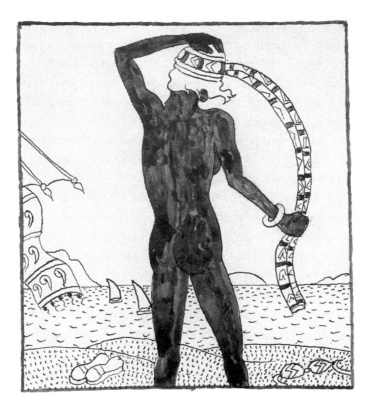

It was a quiet evening in early September when the whole island of Mykonos begins to exhale. In those days tourists had flown back to the north and locals were counting their summer's profits. Only hardier souls stayed on longer then, two of whom Angelos and I sighted as we drank our espressos at a bar in the single inland village of Ano Mera.

"Peter, Jerry, I can hardly believe it?" I said as a sleek SUV pulled up.

"An improvement on the old tub," Jerry said, patting the hood.

"Jerry visited in Berlin and convinced me to come with him," Peter said.

"It had rained for days so I said, why not."

"How long has it been?" I asked. "Thirty years at least."

"When we were healthy and young," Peter said as they sat down.

Peter was a contemporary of mine, a German artist who had some success painting figurative work in the mode of the then fashionable Leipzig school. Jerry had become a real estate broker in Pennsylvania. When we met him he was an itinerant hippy with a rattletrap VW van who travelled from beach to beach making his living by cutting out design motifs from coins and attaching them to chains for necklaces.

Soon we switched from coffee to ouzo, ogled and speculated about our truly beautiful nineteen year old waitress who told us she was from Saloniki, and caught up with our pasts.

"Have you been back here since the old days?" I asked Peter.

"Once, about ten years ago. It was quite a shock. Later if you have time I'll tell you the whole story."

When the beauty and her bar owner boyfriend locked up after about midnight, since we were sitting outside we could stay as long as we wanted.

"Back then," Peter began, "I travelled with nothing but an extra shirt, shorts, underwear and my sketchbook. Life was simple: Cheap food and lodging, inexpensive bars and discos in town, and naked girls from Scandinavia and France on the beach. When we weren't tanning and socializing, I divided my day between drawing and exploring." "I was particularly intrigued by the conical hill that looms over Ano Mera, right there," Peter said pointing up. "Where our friend once saw the centaur," he said as he launched into his story.

A typically brisk breeze was blowing as I ascended a rocky path strewn with potshards to the Venetian castle ruins at its summit. At first I was sure I was alone. However near the top, as I took a leak on a convenient bush, I spotted two youths posing nearly nude, one holding a large amphora on his hip. The other wore nothing but a scarf, wrapped over his shoulder coyly revealing a semi-excited *schwanz*. A few yards away I saw the bottom half of a man with an antique camera. When his head popped out from a black shroud to take a photo by pressing a button on a cable, I saw the photographer was a graybeard. As I watched, still hidden, he said something in Greek and the boys shifted positions.

I have to say I could imagine caressing those smooth young bodies, almost like skinny *madchens*. That night it was hot without a breath of air in my room and I tossed, turned, and woke up with damp bed sheets. The next day, I couldn't keep from again ascending the path to the ruins. This time the models were a male youth and a girl of perhaps eighteen. Without her small breasts she could have been a boy. They were posing in a classical style that led one's eye directly to the girl's fingers lingering against the boy's equipment. I crept closer and was mesmerized by the girl's nymph-like face. This one might have modeled for Botticelli. I was so enraptured that I did not notice dislodging a stone over which I tripped.

"Hello, there," the photographer said with a friendly nod. "Come take a look." The youthful pair kept their position unfazed by my erratic arrival. He had composed them beautifully in reverse on his glass plate.

"I didn't know anyone still used these old view cameras," I said.

"I love details and this is the only camera that satisfies me."

"Do you live here?" I asked.

"I came after the war and never left. I sell my photos in town under the counter, so-to-speak. The people who know history love it." He told me his best seller was a boy sporting an erection standing next to the marble sculpture of a much larger one that still guards the ruins of the Temple of Dionysus on Delos.

The photographer told me his name, Roger Beaumont, and we chatted as he set up his next shot, switching from Greek orders to his models to English effortlessly. We discussed details of glass plates, tintypes and daguerreotypes, and then older artistic techniques — each trying to outdo the other's knowledge. We got along so well Roger invited me to dine with him. He pointed out his house and "garage," where he said he stabled his donkey, just down the hill and across from the convent.

The next evening after hitchhiking on one of the ubiquitous three-wheeled motorized farmer's carts, (the only vehicles on Mykonos at the time apart from its fourteen taxis) I arrived at Roger's door. With a cordial welcome I was introduced to his Greek wife who wiped her hands on her apron before shaking mine. Behind her stood his two daughters, I supposed, who appeared like day and night. Day was the small-breasted radiant creature I had been smitten by yesterday. Night was her older sister, a stringy, sullen creature whose skin had an ashen pallor. The gods had not bestowed attributes fairly on these two.

Before dinner, Roger showed me his studio. In addition to the photographs he made money painting obscene classical scenes on imitation-Greek black ground pottery. His wife was the potter, and for lack of a kiln they were fired at the local bakery. To my untrained eye, they were perfect – had I seen one in a museum I would never have believed it was not Attic fifth century B.C.

The conversation at dinner, like the products that emanated from this home, was mostly about sex. Except for Miss Sullen, even Roger's wife lit up as we dined on a rabbit stew accompanied by local wine. The young beauty flirted with her eyes and in shock I felt her toes rubbing up and down my leg under the table.

"You know Christianity in all its forms especially Orthodox and Roman Catholic has had a nefarious effect on our thinking about the physical," Roger said. "In classical times the body was in sync with the mind. Even going back to Egypt that was true."

"Does that mean I can love 'em and leave 'em?" the radiant one asked, batting her eyes at me.

"What does love have to do with sex," Roger proclaimed with his lips wet with wine. Miss Sullen whose name I now knew, Marta, also attempted to flirt but her leering eyes made it a caricature.

"Mykonos is an outpost of the coming age," Roger said after several more jugs of wine. "Look at the beautiful naked bodies worshipping the sun on our beaches, getting high dancing at night. Why would I want to live anywhere else. I wish I were young enough to take advantage of all the pulchritude," he whispered after his wife left for the kitchen.

Roger was insistent that I spend the night "We have a guest room," he said which made his invitation definitive especially considering all the wine in my system.

It was near the dark of the moon and electricity had not yet wired the town, so I was offered a candle to guide me to my bed. When I blew it out it was pitch dark except for stars spangled in the hot sky outside my unshuttered window. I stripped, lay down on my back, pillowed my head with an arm and luxuriated in a slight breeze that dried the sweat off my body. Just as I was beginning to drowse I heard the latch click and someone entered my room. Before I knew it, the radiant one had planted a kiss on my lips, licked down my chest and stomach and took me in her mouth.

I could not believe my good luck. I figured because of our conversation, whatever would happen next had been sanctioned by my host. I reciprocated. I penetrated and we rocked gently to and fro. I tried to last as long as I could, to let the feeling build. It was like meditation. The sound of our orgasms was hard to muffle as we came slowly but inexorably. Instead of creeping off as I imagined she would, she fell asleep in the crook of my arm.

Sunlight was pouring in the room when I heard a knock that roused me. It was the radiant one, asking if I had a good night. She put her hand over her mouth and giggled as I peered over at my bedmate. It was Miss Sullen, sporting a grin at last. It was like a joke to them. All their faces were wreathed in smiles. When I came out for breakfast, Marta sat down next to me and attempted to hold my hand as if I were her chosen one.

"When will I see you again?" Marta asked trying to curl her fingers around mine, like an octopus, I thought.

"I'm so busy with my work, I'm not sure," I lied.

Usually if I never intend to see a one night stand again, I feel guilty and try to come up with a plausible excuse, in my own mind at least. This time I felt no guilt.

Although I liked Roger, I tried to avoid him because of Marta. After that night I saw her several times in town when she was shopping for things not available in Ano Mera – a category that included everything except food. My curt hellos turned her sullen again and she barely gave me the time of day when she realized I was not to be in her future.

After that summer I headed for Munich to see an art dealer from Berlin who had promised to buy everything I produced in my three months on Mykonos, albeit for a paltry sum. While I was awaiting the ferry to take me to Piraeus with my roll of canvases, I passed an hour at a café on the harbor front with a friend of mine who delighted in talking about, among other things, the vampires which Mykonos used to be famous for. He told me darkly there were rumors that one lived in Ano Mera.

"Is she called Marta?" I asked.

"I don't know her name but I understand they feel their real names should be kept secret. That way you can't cast a spell on them," he replied.

As it happened my career, which had been jogging along making enough money to pay my rent and basic bills but not much more, took a leap upwards about this time.—I became a hit in Germany. Instead of spending summers on Mykonos I was invited to various schlosses and hunting lodges, and on yachts cruising the Rhine or Lake Konstanz. I became a regular at Kampen auf Sylt, a North sea version of St. Tropez for rich Germans where my dealer had a summer gallery.

Eighteen years went by before I returned to the Greek islands. Purely on a fluke I was invited to cruise on the giant white yacht of one of my patrons, a Baron von Krupp. He liked to gather "interesting" people for his voyages. It was boring, he said, if the twenty or so guests he could accommodate were all as gay as he was. His boat was known in the fashionable circles of Ibiza, Monaco, Marbella for having the best parties - it was a feather in anyone's social cap to be invited on board, let alone cruise with him.

We sailed from Venice and apparently I filled the role of the "serious" artist on board. The V.I.P. guests were princelings and princesses from obscure former German principalities, shoe designers, society hostesses – the flotsam of the jet set. The non-V.I.P. contingent made the cut by their beauty – mostly boys just out of their teens but to leaven the loaf, a few girls too. These heavenly creatures could not always be distinguished from the crew. The males were encouraged to wear crotch-revealing white jeans and the tightest striped tee-shirts they could muster, the girls ran around mostly in bikini tops and sarongs.

Our early stops were along the Adriatic Sea's Dalmatian coast – picturesque little Croatian ports like Hvar and Korkula in the process of rediscovery by tourists after the Yugoslavian wars. We spent a day exploring the Roman Emperor Diocletian's palace in Split whose vast ruins served as the basis for the town – later buildings were embedded in its compound like a fabric woven alternately from Roman and medieval yarns.

Another day we anchored off Dubrovnik, an ancient sea-going

city which gave to English the word, "argosy" derived from its former name Ragusa. We sailed into a fjord that pierced the tiny Ruritanian country of Montenegro for miles to reach its chief port, Kotor.

Each day on board was a feast of possibilities as straights and gays teamed up or crossed previously forbidden boundaries. My self-image as a one-woman man took quite a beating when lovemaking evolved into trios and quartets. By the time our ship of fools passed the Gibraltar-like rock of Monemvasia and broached the swells of the Aegean, the ship's doctor was busy dispensing remedies for the illnesses that arise from promiscuity along with the usual antibiotics.

At every landing the Baron's scouts picked up attractive youths to hitch a ride to the next port or if particularly gorgeous, the port after that. By the time we reached Greek waters he had ditched most of the Italians, Croatians and Montenegrans giving each a packet of bank notes and a ticket home and was eager to find new blood. Of course Mykonos was the place for that. The Baron was eager to see his old friends, with whom he shared fond memories of summer escapades on the island before he reached his majority and subsequent inheritance.

I landed there in the first launch along with the Baron eager to see what had happened to Mykonos over almost two decades. I don't have to tell you the most obvious change was the plethora of autos, scooters, even trucks whose presence had necessitated paving roads and building more of them. Then there were the shops. In my day a sandal maker could afford a place on the main shopping street. Now it was a bank. Vengera, a bar we all frequented had become Kasseris, a chic Athenian jeweler, Pierrot's our favorite disco had turned exclusively gay. To service giant cruise ships that now stopped here, cheap souvenir shops proliferated like mushrooms, poisoning the town with plaster Parthenons and refrigerator magnets in the shape of windmills.

Walking down the whitewashed streets I felt as if I was in a movie version of what used to be.

Von Krupp's yacht was scheduled to move and anchor off Elia Beach at noon. As you remember when we spread our towels there in the old days it was a wide stretch of pristine sand at the end of a dusty road. Now umbrellas and wooden chaises covered it military formation style all the way to the water's edge. The simple tavernas with gravel floors and pecking chickens running wild had morphed into chic restaurants, and formerly bare hillsides hosted hotels with swimming pools.

As on every evening we changed into informal but chic attire and met on the afterdeck. The Baron had a thing for white and a good ship's laundry kept everyone in cotton and linen that contrasted so well with the tans we all worked on. Trays of Bellinis were passed around because the chef had found fresh peaches in the market. The human fruits of the scouts were brought on board from rubber Zodiac boats, which noisily docked just below us, wreathing the party in exhaust fumes. The new boys and girls were the usual – raw good looks untempered by taste. Provincial girls, it seemed almost as a rule, tweezed their eyebrows too thin and the boys, despite picture-perfect bodies, sported bad teeth. Their attire, several years' out-of-date, featured tight satin shirts and tiny miniskirts in an odd range of colors, I could see why white was demanded.

The Baron swanned around the deck in full make-up and curly wig that made him a ringer for Caligula. He greeted each new arrival hospitably with the suggestion of a handshake and a stare strong enough to undress them in his mind. All were soon integrated among his friends who asked questions, and wandered away bored before they had completed their answers.

One youth of eighteen or so stood out from the rest. He was thin but muscular and his eyes had long lashes like a girl's. Perhaps it was my narcissism but I felt he resembled me a generation ago before my formerly good looks were larded over with too much good food, drink, and too many late nights. I thought nostalgically of the time when my appearance alone could attract whatever I wanted.

The boy was introduced to me by the Baron as Panos.

"Look at that beautiful hair, not typical for a Greek," he said as he ruffled Panos's bleached blonde locks before he flitted away like a drunken butterfly.

I told Panos that I had spent time on Mykonos years ago. I waxed on how life on the island was so simple then and so perfect for the wallet of an artist at the beginning of his career.

"Do you need a model? I can do that," Panos said with downcast eyes as I described how the island had inspired my work.

"Normally not, but it's worth a try. Tomorrow," I said.

I liked the boy for his appearance halfway between a tawny lion and a waif but also for his shyness. He lacked the grandiose airs attractive youths often assume as compensation for their lack of experience in the grown-up world. Panos went to fetch us fresh drinks. It was a pleasure to watch him wend his way back to me, like a faithful servant carrying two flutes.

We sat beside each other at dinner that night. The Baron had requisitioned the beach restaurant and our large party of perhaps fifty colonized most of it. No one paid attention to other diners as we raucously filled the place with our camaraderie. The evening ended with two lesbians shedding their clothes and inhibitions to perform unspeakable acts with a champagne bottle on a debris-laden table. That night, the Baron decided to extend his stay in Mykonos – "So much fun, and so much game."

When he arrived on a Zodiac the next morning, right on schedule I greeted Panos and set up my drawing utensils. I rarely work from life – everything usually comes directly from my fevered imagination, I like to say. I am drawn to Byzantine icons and

Mogul miniatures where the figures are symbolic, not reflections of reality. I have pontificated many times that in the history of art there have been just a few periods when realistic work has been favored – sometimes in Egypt, in ancient Greece and Rome and from the Renaissance until about one hundred years ago.

"Shall I undress?" Panos asked.

When I saw him blush, I asked him if he had ever modeled before.

"Never for artists. Photographers. A Greek fashion magazine did a photo shoot here last year. I was the urchin next to the princess.

When he disrobed I remarked from his overall tan that he was not a stranger to nude sunbathing. He blushed again. His body was flawless enough that if I rendered it faithfully it would appear idealized.

I made several quick sketches asking him to pose in attitudes I remembered from classical statues, then settled for one that I developed in more detail. After an hour of work our relationship became less stilted and I asked him about his family and upbringing.

"I was raised by my mother. I never knew my father but I had a wonderful grandfather. He was an artist, too. Because he died several years ago there was no money for me to go to school after that."

I showed him my finished sketch and either because he thought it was required or because of the vanity of youth, he oohed and ahhed. I told him it didn't do him justice, but I would give it to him. "It is my Mother's birthday soon. This will make a perfect gift," he said. "You must come to my house and we will both present it to her." Since it turned out he lived in Ano Mera and I was curious to see if the village had changed, I accepted his invitation.

The next day was breezy and cool. After a Zodiac from the

yacht dropped me off at the beach where Panos waited, we walked to Ano Mera – a distance of perhaps two miles. I was comfortable in Panos' presence and think he felt easy with me despite the vast difference of our ages and inequity of our lives. I imagined I could be his mentor, but not here. If he remained, Panos would end up as a waiter with a heavy wife and kids, chasing tourist women until he too became fat and indolent. His days would end watching ferries come and go while he played backgammon in a harborside café. Handsome Greek boys faded fast on their own turf.

When he pointed out the road to his house, I remembered it well. Now it was paved but the buildings looked the same. By now I realized his artist grandfather from England had to be the artist and photographer I had known. I was greeted by his mother shrouded in black in the old peasant style with a nut-brown face wrinkled by years of outdoor work. I knew immediately who she was. The old woman stared at my face as if she had seen a ghost. I wondered how she could be so weather-beaten when she had a son so young.

She shuffled into the kitchen and pointed to a chair, but before I could sit down I noticed several photographs hanging on the wall next to a calendar featuring the Virgin Mary. They were faded but I recognized Roger Beaumont, the two sisters, beautiful and plain, and his long suffering wife, just like this one.

"What happened to her?" I asked. The old woman crossed herself as I pointed to the beautiful one.

"She often stayed with my family but she was a neighbor. I never met her," Panos said. "The other one is my mother."

A stray and shocking thought arose in my mind. Could it be the closeness I felt for Panos was the love of father for son? How would he feel finally knowing his real father I fantasized. I could show Panos the world, make him somebody.

Later we had a polite cup of sludgy Greek coffee at a café across from the village's chief tourist attraction, a monastery staffed with a single monk whose sole task was to solicit contributions. How could I recount the entire story of my deception? I ended up simply telling him I knew his grandfather and his mother many years ago. I'm not sure he believed me. I was certain his mother would never have breathed a word about what happened.

Impulsively I tendered Panos a wad of euros which he refused almost acting as it was an insult before calling a taxi to take me back to the yacht. "The sketch is my payment," he said.

When I arrived at the port there was no boat. After frantically asking around I found the harbormaster's office next to the dock where ferries landed. "Weren't you contacted?" a man there said. "The *meltemi* is blowing up to Bofor Seven and the Baron decided to avoid it by shipping out to Santorini. You can join the boat there."

Thank god I had kept my cash.

BLIND LOVE

For once we were having our evening ouzo snug in Angelos' windmill, the first of five counting from the sea. Because of a wide stairway outside down to the town whose size serves no reasonable purpose today, it is speculated that there was an acropolis here in classical times. "Perhaps we are imbibing on the very site of a temple dedicated to Dionysus the god of wine and disorder," Angelos said as he raised his glass.

Above us a strong wind clacked the ropes that tied down the windmill's furled sails. Except for tourists on budget tours, the season was over and it was just a matter of time before the Sahara high that kept this part of the Aegean dry and sunny from June to September would retreat back to Africa.

After our first drink we took a look outside. The view from Angelos rocky terrace was a panorama of the whole port from hills covered with white villas to a lit-up ferry arriving from the mainland.

"You see those houses being sprayed by the high waves tonight," Angelos pointed. "It reminds me of a scandal involving an artist and a blind girl who lived down there."

"Tell me more, but do it inside," I said as I felt the wind blowing right through the loose weave of my fisherman's sweater.

The artist was called Ethan Templeton and he arrived here intending to stay just a few weeks, then move on to some other interesting place, such as Capri or Taormina, but Mykonos reeled him in like a big fish. Within a short time he had found lodgings in the Little Venice neighborhood called Alefkandra, that line of buildings I just pointed out whose foundations are lapped by the sea. It is said they were erected by homesick Venetians who ruled this island in the Archipelago, as they called the Greek islands, for several centuries until 1537 when the Turkish Admiral Barbarossa conquered it. Later such proximity to the sea facilitated the secret unloading of cargo stolen by the corsairs who used Mykonos as a home base.

All of this added romance for Ethan who was more than pleased with his large bare white-washed room. Its ceiling was composed of cross-beams holding up woven raffia like a tent. With its large paned window overlooking the Aegean, the islands of Delos, Tinos and further away the smudge that was Syros, it was a place to dream. At night a briny breeze and the lap of waves put Ethan to sleep. The sun set directly over the sea in the middle of his window and he frequently invited friends over to watch it turn orange and pink and then disappear into the misty gray horizon.

In the room where Ethan painted, his palette lightened to match the contrasts between the dark sea and the white cubist architecture which defines Mykonos. These dominants were accented by morning glories of an intense blue-purple he'd never seen before, the pinks of oleander, the bright oranges, yellows and greens of fruit and beach towels.

He rarely saw inhabitants of the other rooms, and when he did, he wondered where the landlord found them. Most were disabled in some way – lame, half-blind, stooped, afflicted by an unfortunate fate in one way or another. It made Ethan wonder why he had been offered a room. The landlord himself was an odd fellow who liked to claim he was descended from Venetian nobility, and barely came up to Ethan's chest. Upon discovering his tenant was an artist, he insisted Ethan pay for his room via a portrait. Ethan normally was not interested in portraits – Arcadian scenes and icons were his thing – but he relented. He challenged himself to paint the landlord like a secular icon with an elaborate border.

Ethan's life that summer on Mykonos evolved into a pleasurable rhythm as unchanged every day as the weather—painting mornings, afternoons on the beach chasing girls, evenings at bars and discos in town with or without the nymphs he'd caught. Too bad youth is so fleeting, he thought, otherwise he could live this life forever.

For days, Ethan put off starting the landlord's portrait. There was something about the landlord's face that bothered him. Perhaps it was just that he preferred to paint the smooth curves of females. "If we don't start soon I'll have to give your room to someone else" the landlord said one morning as Ethan passed him on the stoop. Ethan still did not understand why to the landlord having his portrait painted was more important than rent money but they agreed that sittings would take place twice a week until his visage was immortalized. Ethan told him that he worked in the old fashioned medium of egg tempera so it would take some time to complete.

The days passed slowly as Ethan devoted as much time as he could to more inspiring subjects, but put in enough drudgery on the portrait to satisfy the landlord that he was making progress. As he worked, Ethan noticed that the paint would dry darker than expected; perhaps he was not used to the bright light of Mykonos and tried to compensate, or there was something in the salty air he thought. Whatever, it caused his subject's face to look menacing in a way he did not intend.

The landlord said that he had no problem with dark. "Sometimes I feel Mykonos has too much light. Aren't the works of old masters dark?" he said.

Ethan explained. "Oil paint darkens with time, but time measured in centuries. Five hundred-year-old paintings in my technique of egg tempera are just as bright as the day they were painted. Look at Duccio or Sassetta."

"Hmm," said the landlord. "So you like it here?"

"It is paradise. I'm dreading the day I'll have to leave, or the weather changes."

"What if I offered you a way to stay? And not just for the summer," the landlord added.

"How would that work?" Ethan asked.

"It is complicated in the details—a lot of paperwork—but to put it simply, we would have to find someone willing to die in your place."

"Like Jesus?"

"What does Jesus have to do with it?" the landlord asked with petulance in his voice. "I'll see if I can find someone for you."

Ethan lay on the beach that day trying to imagine what kind of person would sacrifice his life for another. But it didn't take long for a modern martyr to appear. She showed up the next day with sunglasses and a white cane.

"Let me introduce one of my tenants, Monica Trefusis." She was pale and wan, unusual for Mykonos but had an attraction that grew on Ethan as he studied her long-lashed non-seeing eyes and slight figure.

"The landlord here tells me you are looking for someone who is out of their senses. That might be me," she said and smiled. I hear you are an artist. What do you paint?"

Ethan realized the futility of attempting to explain a landscape or a face. That was why he painted, but he tried because the girl appeared intelligent and despite her disability, quite attractive.

"It's hard to describe. Right now I am inspired by old icons-they have an extra dimension of feeling. What I'm trying to create are icons that are not religious – like beautiful women or Arcadian idylls. Something else to worship," he said with a grin she could not see. "That's a tall order, to take the religious out of the icon. You are ambitious." "I hope in my next life I'll be able to see them for myself," Monica said.

"I've done my job. I imagine you both can carry on without me," said the landlord as he bowed out.

When the door closed, Ethan asked again why she would accept such a one-sided deal. "Are you depressed?"

"Not at all. Knowing the due date, I believe the remaining days will be more poignant and beautiful, don't you think?"

"You could also have a sense of dread," Ethan said.

Perhaps her view on the matter is more profound because of her disability, Ethan imagined. He had read that the loss of one sense enhanced the others.

The landlord appeared that evening with a contract for him to sign. One clause stipulated that Ethan and Monica must get to know each other before the event in question occurred. Another clause predicated that its fulfillment would take place in September on the neighboring island of Santorini, chosen because of the high cliffs that towered over its currently inactive caldera.

"What will you, the landlord get out if it?" asked Ethan.

"Ten percent of all your earnings in perpetuity. You see I have faith in you."

"What does Monica get out of your deal for committing suicide?" Ethan shuddered when he realized the implications of what he put so bluntly.

"Monica will have done something good. For herself. For her karma. She will also have done something very good for you."

The last clause said that Ethan and Monica must be in daily contact until the event.

"Why is that?" Ethan asked.

"It will be to your benefit. When Monica's parents died they left her a considerable sum of money. She can help pay for you in the time she has left and afterwards we'll split what remains fifty-fifty." In a spirit of mock seriousness because deep down he couldn't imagine the contract was real, Ethan signed it.

The next morning his work on the landlord's portrait progressed more easily than before and in a few days it was finished. A disquieting note was provided by the cleaning maid who upon seeing it grasped the pendant of a cross that hung around her neck and splayed her fingers forward with it as if to counter the evil eye. Even Ethan had noticed how close his portrait of the landlord resembled the popular image of the devil.

Monica took to sitting in Ethan's room during his working mornings and proved to be wonderful company. When she recounted vivid stories of her life, while he painted his work turned out better than ever. His colors and forms became clearer, his ideas flew from sketch to painting as if they had wings.

When she was in his room she took to wearing a colorful

blindfold instead of her sunglasses – she said her sightless eyes were not for anyone to see. Somehow she knew when he watched her and faintly smiled. Usually she wore simple dresses with short sleeves, but as the weather turned sultry in August she appeared wearing just an artfully tied sarong and sandals.

As they became more intimate, Ethan prevailed upon Monica to partially and later fully disrobe to serve as a model. Since what Ethan could see was looking more and more desirable it took an effort of will not to touch her. As the days progressed, what he initially observed as a good body and face when she posed and he sketched became his ideal perfect woman, his muse. He lost interest in his beach afternoons.

One morning he could stand it no more. The beautiful and charming savior sitting nude across from him as he played with his charcoal stick was too much. He lay it down, crossed the room, kissed her on the lips, took her in hand and placed her on his bed. There was no resistance. From that day on when he finished his work they made love. Often they would lie coupled inside each other for an hour feeling a quiet ecstasy that dimmed the passage of time.

The date scheduled for their fateful trip drew closer.

One fine day in late September when the flood of tourists had ebbed back to their gray cities in the north, Ethan and Monica boarded a ferry headed to Santorini. They travelled light as if they would be gone a day or two. When they arrived on the volcanic island, which hosted a prosperous community in ancient times before it exploded and created a tsunami wave giant enough to extinguish all of Minoan civilization, they had no trouble finding a room overlooking the sea a thousand or more feet below.

They spent their first evening drinking margaritas on their terrace as the ancient sun drummed down to the horizon in barbaric fluorescent colors. Without conversing much they ate a last supper together. After supper they took a walk so Ethan could see the lay of the land.

That night they made love for the last time. Their passion was intense as if they were attempting to hold off eternity itself. Afterwards they held hands until the rosy pink fingers of dawn stretched over the caldera.

"Are you sure you want to go through with this?" Ethan asked her as they dressed.

"It is my fate," she said.

"We are happy together. We can be happy together," Ethan said. But her mind was made up.

They exited their room, walked past sleepy honeymooners breakfasting on spectacular verandas and up the pebble-paved path that served as the main road as it zigged and zagged along the lip of the submerged volcano's crater. A cruise boat below looked like a toy. Cable cars were already climbing and descending the cliff face bringing tourists for their hours atop the world. Ethan and Monica found a place to step off the path. They crossed a small sloping field of loose dirt and gravel interspersed with cactus to the very edge.

"It is time to say goodbye," Monica said.

"Are you sure?" Ethan asked. He reached out to embrace her one last time but as fate would have it, he slipped on the gravel and his body pushed into hers. "Wait, wait" he said as if his words could stop her as she fell over backwards and along with the clatter of stones plunged down. He peered over the edge and saw nothing. The cliff was so steep that her body must already be fathoms deep in the water. He turned away. He could hardly see his way back to the hotel through his tears.

He found out later, when the police came for him in his room, that a Japanese tourist had videoed the whole event. And Monica was still alive. She had fallen onto a ledge invisible from above. Her descent had been arrested by shrubs that clung tenaciously to the cliff wall and though she was hurt she was not dead. She was rushed by helicopter to a hospital in Athens but it was too late. The arduous task of roping rescuers to clamber down to the ledge – actually the remains of a house that an earthquake in the fifties had dislodged – took too long and now along with her blindness her brain was damaged. She could not see *or* speak.

The angle of the tourist's camera made it appear that Ethan had pushed Monica. Police like hard evidence and for them, the angle was not open to interpretation. They would not let him meet with Monica.

A lawyer recommended to Ethan by the U.S. Consulate in Athens convinced the local police to contact their counterparts in Mykonos and find the landlord on the off chance he might help explain Monica's own desires.

Several days later they received word back that in their cataloging of what remained in Monica's and Ethan's rooms there was no evidence of a deal. The landlord had decamped for Tirana and wouldn't return until the following Easter, his Albanian housekeeper said. Although she told the police she was under strict instructions not to let anyone into his private quarters, fearing the authorities might look into her own illegal status in Greece if she didn't, she relented.

Everything was in spic and span order but oddly there were none of the framed photos most people scatter around of relatives, friends and themselves. On a prominently placed easel was a painting of just an elaborate border. The center of it was a kind of tarry black void.

Fortunately for Ethan the Japanese tourist who had left his video with the police was back in his homeland and could not be found. When the prosecuting attorneys were assembling their evidence, they found the tape like the portrait had also turned blank. The only evidence they had was testimony from various people who'd seen it when it was still legible. Ethan's lawyer reminded them that since they were not eyewitnesses, their recollections could easily be refuted as faulty or even thrown out.

Prosecution was finally declined but Ethan was required to leave Greece as a *persona non grata*. It was shortly before Christmas when Ethan found out Monica was living at a home for disabled people near San Francisco.

He approached her as she sat under a pergola of wisteria in a wheelchair. He carried violets – if she could not see or speak she could still smell he reasoned. When he touched her hand she squeezed his. There was an upwelling of love in his heart as he realized she knew it was him. She was not dead. He was not immortal. They would live together happily ever after.

"Angelos, that last part sounds made up," I said. "How do you know what happened in California if Ethan could never return?"

"You caught me," Angelos said, as I watched the clear ouzo clouding up as he replenished my drink. "Don't you agree that ending the story with Ethan just being expelled from Greece is a bit flat?"

"Yes, but it also makes me wonder how many other embellishments there are to your stories." Angelos ignored a justification. "Did I ever tell you about the German girl called Rapunzel who one summer lived up in the tower bedroom, between my windmill's cogs," Angelo said.

"I might believe you if her name was something else," I replied.

ABOUT THE AUTHOR

© Renate McKnight

The appeal of Thomas McKnight's prints, paintings, and posters place him in a small group of contemporary artists whose work is instantly recognizable. Be it a carnival in Venice, a sun-drenched street in Greece, a well -furnished room, a tropical beach, or a mythological scene, McKnight's vision brings dreams to life.

"I try to integrate what is real about a place or thing with its underlying truth - that is, its invisible soul," muses the artist. "In the process, I try to create a symbolic reality that can serve as a catalyst for emotions - nostalgia, joy, the sadness of time passing." According to New York Times critic Gene Thornton, McKnight's work presents "vision of earthly happiness that are almost celestial. It is the vision of earthly paradise that exists in the here and now."

Born in 1941 in Lawrence, Kansas, Thomas McKnight grew up in the suburbs of Montreal, New York, and Washington, D.C.

After receiving his Bachelor's Degree from Wesleyan University, he studied art history at Columbia University. He served in Korea with the army for two years, and later worked for Time Magazine.

Since devoting himself to painting full time in 1972, McKnight's work has been exhibited throughout the United States, Europe, and Japan. His prints have appeared in numerous movies and television shows, including on Sally's bedroom wall in When Harry Met Sally. McKnight's work is represented in the permanent collection of the Metropolitan Museum in New York and Washington's Smithsonian Institute as well as the New Britain Museum of Art in Connecticut.

In 1988 McKnight's print Constitution was chosen as the official image of the U.S. Constitution Bicentennial. Longtime McKnight fans, the Clintons asked the artist to create an image for the Presidential Christmas card in 1994, 1995, and 1996. His images of the White House Red, Green, and Blue Rooms have now appeared on almost a million cards sent out worldwide. In 2023 Waterbury Connecticut's Mattatuck Museum presented a large show of McKnight's mythologically oriented work.

Seven books of McKnight's art have been published (two in Japan), most recently Thomas McKnight's Arcadia. He was commissioned by the city of Kobe, Japan, in 1993 to create a series of paintings to serve as the centerpiece for two-year celebration of its tricentennial. This was accompanied by a retrospective of his work at the Kobe Art Museum.

Thomas McKnight paints daily in his studio in Litchfield, Connecticut where he lives with his Austrian born wife Renate. For more information about Thomas McKnight, contact us at thomasmcknight.com.

Printed in the USA
CPSIA information can be obtained
at www.ICGtesting.com
CBHW021746230524
8975CB00003B/140

9 781636 830650